ONE
TOO
MANY

ONE TOO MANY

PEGGIE C. MOODY

LUTTERWORTH PRESS
GUILDFORD SURREY ENGLAND

First paperback edition 1969
Reprinted 1981

COPYRIGHT © 1941 LUTTERWORTH PRESS
ALL RIGHTS RESERVED

ISBN 0 7188 1592 0

Printed in Great Britain by
Fletcher & Son Ltd, Norwich

CONTENTS

Chapter I

NUMBER THIRTY-ONE

MAIDA Jackson entered the recreation-room and was immediately accosted by a chorus of voices inquiring:

" Is anything up ? "

" Yes," she replied, " a new addition to our ranks."

Then, forestalling an avalanche of questions, she hastened to add:

" I may as well tell every one about her at the same time."

Maida was head girl at The Elms, and had just returned from Miss Martin's study, to which she had been summoned a short time before. She was tall and attractive-looking, with fair hair and blue eyes, and had only one more year at school. She now stood with her back to the fire and raised her voice, so that all in the room could hear.

" Listen to me, everybody, for a moment," she said.

The juniors stopped talking and drew near.

" I have just come from the Head's study,

where she told me that there was a new girl arriving to-morrow."

Here she was interrupted by one of the seniors.

"But there isn't any room for her, Maida; we've got thirty."

"Well, we're going to have thirty-one."

"Then it isn't fair, Maida," broke in one of the juniors, "because a great friend of ours, Mrs. Wickham, wanted to send Nancy to The Elms this term, and Miss Martin wrote saying she hadn't room. Nancy was awfully fed up about it."

"Aunt Bee never takes more than thirty," asserted Judy Martin, the harum-scarum niece of the Head.

"She is making an exception, then, in this case," replied Maida, "and certainly the circumstances do seem exceptional, for the new girl, Penelope Swanson, is coming all the way from China."

"Penelope! did you say, Maida? Oh, help!" remarked Judy. "And is she a Chinee? I shall call her Chink."

"You'll do nothing of the kind," returned Maida sharply.

"Miss Martin spoke of her as 'Pen', so I suppose that is what she is called."

"Well, pennies chink, don't they?" murmured the irrepressible Judy.

Maida looked at her severely and addressed

the amused company.

"It seems that she is the daughter of old friends of Miss Martin's, who are missionaries in China. She is bound to feel strange, especially as she is coming from a large school. The Head wants us to be friendly and nice to her—as, of course, we shall be," she added.

"Where is she going to sleep?" inquired Dora Woods, a girl of fourteen, and a great admirer of Judy's.

"In room number eight, I think."

"Oh, I say!" exclaimed Judy, shaking her carroty curls and pulling a long face, "that's too bad."

Number eight was where she and Dora slept, along with the two Westcott girls, Ruth and Eileen.

"She'll take us for heathen and try to convert us, I know; she's sure to be a prig. Why on earth should Aunt Bee introduce such a disturbing element into our midst?"

"Don't be silly," commanded Maida; but in spite of herself she had to smile at the look of consternation on Judy's face.

"How old is she?" inquired another voice.

"Fourteen."

"When does she arrive?"

"The boat is due to-morrow morning, but I don't know when she will arrive here."

" Who is meeting her, Maida?" Judy asked.

" I really couldn't say; I have told you all I know," and Maida turned to warm herself at the fire, for, although it was the beginning of the summer term, Easter had fallen early and the evenings were quite chilly.

" Let's hope Aunt Bee will go herself, for that would mean no scripture lesson to-morrow morning for us," muttered Judy. " One should always look for the bright lining to every cloud, so they say."

The girls laughed, but Maida disregarded this remark, and the juniors returned to their end of the room to discuss the matter among themselves.

The recreation-room at The Elms, running the whole length of one of the two houses of which the school was composed, was a very attractive place. There were folding doors in the middle which made it possible to convert it into two separate rooms, and one end was considered the property of the seniors, those of sixteen and over, while in the other the juniors spent their free hours. The school had been moved recently to Redheath, and Miss Martin had been fortunate in securing two semi-detached houses within a few minutes' walk of the Common, a wide expanse of hill and dale, to the north of London. It was not a large school, thirty boarders being the greatest number Miss Martin had ever taken. Their ages varied from twelve to seventeen. The staff consisted of three resident teachers besides the Head; Miss Edgar, the English mistress; Miss Miles, who taught languages; and Miss Lawson, who took mathematics. Miss Martin taught science and Scripture herself, and there were visiting teachers for music and art.

While the girls were discussing the news which Maida had brought them, Miss Martin was talking to Miss Edgar in her study. Small and slim, with large grey eyes and wavy hair, there was something about Miss Barbara Martin which made people look at her more than once. She had what is sometimes called "presence", and the staff at the school, no less than the girls, were aware of a rare quality in her which they would have found it hard to describe.

"I have just had word from the shipping office that the boat from Shanghai is due at Tilbury to-morrow morning at eleven o'clock," she said. "I think that, in spite of your kind suggestion to meet Penelope, Miss Edgar, I had better go myself; she will feel less strange and forlorn if she sees a face she knows."

"I quite agree," replied Miss Edgar. "Poor child, what a journey to have taken by herself! How old did you say she was?"

"She must be fourteen now. The last time her parents were home was six years ago; she was eight then, I remember, and too small to come to us here. You see I have only her mother's cable saying she was sending her to me. The letter with explanations, which was to follow, has not arrived yet, and I am beginning to realize how little I really know about her. Mrs. Swanson and I were at school together," she added.

Miss Edgar listened with interest.

" Has Penelope any relations in England?" she asked.

" I think she must have some; but not any near ones; her grandparents on both sides are gone, I know. Things are so unsettled in China just now that I suppose her parents have thought it best to send her home. I am proposing to put up another bed in number eight room for her. I must speak to Mrs. Philips about it. May I trouble you to ask her to come to me now? Thank you, Miss Edgar."

Mrs. Philips was housekeeper at The Elms and Miss Martin's right hand in all matters concerning the comfort of the girls and Staff; indeed in domestic matters Miss Martin counted herself very fortunate, as she had for cook one who had been connected with the family for many years, and who had left the Martin home to help " Miss Barbara ", as she always called her, in her new venture of establishing a school for girls.

" There is plenty of space for another bed in

number eight room," Mrs. Philips agreed, when the Head raised the question, " and there is that extra dressing-table and chest upstairs in the box-room; the only thing we shall need is rails for cubicle curtains. If we telephone at once, the man will come and put them up to-morrow, I am sure. What time will she arrive?"

" In the morning, but it will probably be after-noon before we get out here, as I shall have to see her luggage through the customs," replied Miss Martin. " Then I may leave all the preparations to you, Mrs. Philips, may I? Thank you."

When she was alone again, Miss Martin turned to a letter which Mary, the maid, had just brought in. It was the one she had been expecting from Mrs. Swanson.

My Dear Bee (Miss Martin read),

By this time you will have received our cable saying that we are sending Pen home to you. You see, we have taken you at your word and believe you meant what you said when you promised to help us at any time. I do hope this letter will arrive before the child, but outgoing mails are very uncertain now. You will gather from the address at the top of the page that we have not been able to go to Shanghai to see Pen off; it is rather hard on her to be bundled home so suddenly, but she is travelling in the charge of some very nice people, a Mr. and Mrs. Newland. And what makes it easier for her is that her great friend, Nan Murdoch, is going home to an aunt and uncle in Glasgow, and is to be on the same boat. In fact, I believe that the Newlands are shepherding quite a number of boys and girls who are being sent home at this time. You see, in the present state of affairs, the authorities think it wise that as many as possible of the pupils in the school at Wu-lu should go home. Their resources may be strained to the utmost to keep the school going and look after those whose parents can't arrange for them to leave.

In Pen's case it only means ante-dating her homegoing by a year, for, as you know, our furlough falls due next Spring. She was to study for General Certificate; but perhaps now it might be wiser for her to try a scholarship, as she wants to teach. Anyhow, you will know best how to advise her, and she will be guided by your decision.. I can't begin to tell you what it means to us to know that she is to be with you, and we are tremendously grateful. I do hope she will get on well at The Elms. She always talks of you as "Aunt Barbara"; but, of course, knows she mustn't call you that in school! She has changed tremendously these last few years, so I enclose a photograph, taken in the winter when she was home. I am sorry she is in Chinese dress, but she loves to wear it in the holidays. I do hope she will settle down quickly and get on with the other girls; I know she will miss the life at Wu-lu very much.

Then followed some business details and general news.

Miss Martin gazed thoughtfully at the photograph that was enclosed in the letter. She saw a tall slim girl with short hair, dressed in Chinese trousers and coat; her forehead was broad, her eyes set widely apart and she was laughing. In her arms she held a tiny kitten.

"Changed! I should think you have," Miss Martin said, addressing the photograph. "Well, Pen, I hope you will be happy with us, if not for your own sake, then for your mother's."

Chapter 2

A DOUBTFUL WELCOME

IT was a beautiful evening with the stars shining clear and bright as Penelope Swanson and Nan Murdoch hung over the rail on the second-class deck of the S.S. *Ranpura*. They had experienced a bad tossing in the Bay of Biscay, but the Channel was calmer and the following day would bring them into port. Nan gazed at the stars.

" Isn't Orion fine to-night?" she remarked; " I'm glad he will always be there."

Pen assented dreamily.

" Wouldn't it be lovely always to see a great expanse of sky like this?" Nan continued. " You never seem to get it anywhere except at sea; not even at dear old Wu-lu."

" Oh Nan," cried Pen, " I do wish we hadn't had to leave."

" So do I," agreed her friend. " We'll never, never forget the jolly times we had there, will we? And it makes it worse having to leave at this time, when China is in such bad straits."

" Much worse," replied Pen, " it hardly bears

thinking about. What school will you be going to in Glasgow, do you think?"

"The Glasgow High, if possible," laughed Nan. "Aunt Mary was there herself and thinks no school comes anywhere near it."

"I wish I were coming with you," sighed Pen.

"So do I," declared Nan fervently. "But I expect you will like The Elms all right, and you know Miss Martin, that's always something."

They fell silent after this, both being occupied with thoughts of their own, until a voice broke in on their reverie.

"Dear me! are you two girls still on deck? It's high time you were off to bed."

It was Mrs. Newland who had accosted them.

"It's such a perfect night," cried Nan, "and the last one. Can't we stay up a little longer?"

"Here is Mr. Newland," broke in Pen. "Oh, do let us walk round the deck again."

On condition that it should be once only, the four of them set off, arm in arm.

"You will be very glad to get rid of us all to-morrow," Pen said.

Mrs. Newland laughed.

"Not exactly," she returned, "but I dare say we shall breathe a sigh of relief when you are all safely handed over to your relations and friends. Will you know Miss Martin, Pen?"

" I think so, although it is a long time since I saw her; but Mother said she should send her a photograph of me, so perhaps she may do the recognizing first. That is if the letter has arrived, of course. Everything was done in such a hurry that we hadn't time to arrange to wear a rosette, as Nan has planned to do."

" I hope you will manage to see something of one another, here at home," Mr. Newland remarked.

He had grown very fond of these two girls during the voyage.

" We must," declared Pen, " although we are going to be horribly far away. But surely we will be able to spend some part of our holidays together."

" Of course we will," asserted Nan.

When their promenade of the deck was completed Mrs. Newland sent them off to bed, saying that the next day would be both an exciting and a tiring one.

Although the boat was due at Tilbury at eleven o'clock, it was nearly two before she arrived. The passengers crowded round the rails eager to scan the tender as it put off from the quay. Mr. and Mrs. Newland were shepherding the young ones of their flock, so Pen and Nan undertook to watch for their own friends and, when they arrived, take them to report to the Newlands in the saloon, where they had arranged to hand over their charges.

"What a squash!" exclaimed Pen, as the tender drew alongside. "Will people ever spot their friends among that crowd?"

"Some have already," answered Nan. "Look how they are waving. And, Pen, I do believe I see Aunt Mary. Look! behind that stout woman in the stern; do you see her rosette?"

Nan tried to attract the woman's attention, and Pen scanned the faces of those she could see without, however, recognizing anyone. By this time there was quite a hubbub on deck as friends exchanged greetings with friends, and Nan, seeing her aunt step on board, rushed forward to meet her. She led her over to where Pen still hung over the rail, and after speaking together for a few minutes, Nan took her down to the saloon.

Pen watched the stream of people coming on to the boat, then noticed a small woman emerge from behind a very tall man, take something from her bag, glance at it and put it back. Pen concluded that it was a mirror. A feeling of loneliness was creeping over her now that Nan had left. A few minutes later the woman she had idly speculated on stepped on deck, looked about her in an alert way and, noticing the young girl standing by herself at the rail, made straight for her.

"Even if I had not seen a recent photograph of

you," she said, her face lighting up, " I should have known you, Pen, from the likeness to your mother." She kissed Pen.

Pen's heart warmed.

" I don't know that I would have recognized you, Aunt Barbara," she said shyly.

" That is not to be wondered at; six years is a long time, and even then I only saw you once or twice, not nearly as often as I saw your parents. Besides, I took a glance at the photograph your mother sent to me, just before I came on board."

" Oh!" Pen said, " then I saw you; but I thought you were looking at a mirror."

Miss Martin laughed.

" Well, you were wrong."

" I'm so glad Mother's letter has arrived," Pen said. " She wasn't sure that it would get here before me."

Miss Martin glanced at her. Had the child been wondering whether she would get a welcome?

" Yes, it arrived last night, and I am very glad, Pen, that your mother and father have sent you to me; they would know how pleased I should be to have you."

The grateful look that came into Pen's eyes confirmed Miss Martin's suspicion that the matter had been causing anxiety.

" Now," she continued briskly, " we had better

see the friends you have been travelling with, and then make arrangements about your luggage."

There were a few last words with Nan as they went ashore, promises made to write regularly, and the two friends separated. After seeing Pen's luggage through the customs and arranging for the heavy pieces to be sent on to the school, Miss Martin hired a taxicab to take them out to Redheath. On the way she told Pen about the school and encouraged her to talk about her parents.

"There is no fighting going on just now where they are," Pen said, "but you never know when there may be again. Dad says there is nothing to be anxious about, but I can't help worrying a bit; it seems like deserting them to come to England like this, instead of going to them."

"You must not think that," replied Miss Martin. "By coming home you are relieving them of great anxiety, and you must try to help them by being happy with us. That is what they wish."

When they arrived at The Elms, afternoon classes were going on, so Miss Martin took Pen up to number eight room and showed her where she was to sleep.

"Your cubicle curtains are not up yet," she explained. "I hoped the man would have come to fix the rail this morning; however, Mrs. Philips, our housekeeper, will give you screens meanwhile. Now upack your luggage, and then come down to my sitting-room for a cup of tea. It is on the next floor at the end of the passage."

Pen looked at the beds in the four cubicles and wondered what her room-mates would be like. If only Nan had been one of them! After putting away her things in the chest of drawers beside her bed, she made her way downstairs and knocked at the door of the room Miss Martin had indicated. When, after the second knock, she still received no answer, she thought she had better discover whether it was the right room, so cautiously opened the door. On finding that it was, she entered, made her way past arm-chairs covered in gay cretonnes over to the big bay window and gazed out. She saw a long garden laid out with rose-beds and flower-plots, while at the end was what looked like a tennis court. Another garden ran parallel to it. She was still looking out of the window when Miss Martin came in, followed by a maid carrying a tea-tray.

" I see that you have found your way," she said. " Come and sample some of the good things Mary has brought in; then we must have a chat, and at supper I shall introduce you to the girls."

Pen who was dreading that ordeal, was only too glad to have this respite, and she wondered whether Aunt Barbara was always so understanding. She asked her about her school life at Wu-lu, at Wu-lu, and expressed surprise that the number of pupils was so large.

"Four hundred!" she exclaimed, "then I am afraid you will find us a very small community her, for we are only thirty."

Judging from what Pen told her about her classes at Wu-lu, the Head thought she would be in the Fourth Form.

"I do hope you will get on well," she said. "And, Pen, I want you to feel that you can come to me at any time and ask me about anything. Out of school hours, I see no reason why you should not continue to call me Aunt Barbara; it will be more home-like. That is what Judy does," she added. "She is my niece, and her parents are abroad. I hope you two will be friends; you are about the same age."

At this moment there was a thumping at the door.

"That must be Prince," Miss Martin said. "Just open the door for him, will you?"

Pen jumped up and, on her opening the door, a big Chow walked in.

"Oh, you darling!" Pen cried.

"He keeps himself rather aloof," remarked his mistress. "I would describe him as proud, but Judy will not allow me to do so. She is devoted to him. He will take his own time to sum you up; just take no notice of him. When he has made up his mind regarding you he will admit you to his circle of friends, I hope."

Prince was already sniffing round Pen's chair, and she, exercising deliberate restraint, refrained from touching him; but she spoke to him.

" I have just come from your country," she said. " I love it and shall miss it dreadfully; but you will help me by reminding me of home."

Prince looked at her solemnly with his soft brown eyes, then laid a paw on her knee. Pen put her hand over it and said, " Thank you," and the dog stalked to the fireplace and lay down.

" You are highly honoured, Pen," remarked Miss Martin; " I have never known him make friends so quickly."

In spite of the Head's kindness, supper was just as much an ordeal as Pen had feared. She sat next to Miss Martin at one of the long tables, and felt that thirty pairs of eyes were fixed curiously on her, and she was greatly relieved when all rose and Miss Martin said Grace. After being introduced to the Staff she was put into Maida's charge.

" I shan't need to introduce you again," Maida said, opening the door of the recreation-room, " but I expect you would like to know the girls with whom you are to share a bedroom," and she led Pen to a group by the fire. " Miss Martin called you Pen, she began, " so I suppose that is what you like to be called; here are Ruth and Eileen Westcott, Dora Woods and Judy Martin." She pointed to each in turn.

Pen looked with particular interest at Judy, who returned her glance with one difficult to define, and the newcomer felt somehow that the jolly-looking girl with the carroty curls was not going to be very friendly. But they were all polite and tried to make conversation. She was rather tired and still felt the motion of the ship, so she was glad when a bell rang and Eileen told her it was bedtime.

"We have half an hour before one of the mistresses comes to see that lights are out," she said.

Pen soon discovered that she had become a member of a lively room, and it was quite evident that Judy was the moving spirit. In the ceaseless conversation three names occurred frequently. They were "Eddie," "Smiles," and "Gracie". She wondered who they were. She had just knelt down to say her prayers when one of her screens was pulled aside and Judy popped her head round.

"Oh, sorry!" she muttered, and retired to her own cubicle.

Then in a stage whisper she called over to Dora in the next bed:

"I told you so! She's on her knees and there's

a Bible beside her on the table. I bet that in a jiffy she'll be out in the middle of the room, preaching."

Dora giggled, and Pen buried her face deeper in her hands.

Chapter 3

WAR DECLARED

IN spite of a feeling of loneliness and a great longing for Nan's companionship, Pen did not sleep too badly that first night at The Elms.

Judy's ridicule, however, made her feel more forlorn than anything else had done. She did not wake up at the usual early hour to which life in the East had accustomed her, the rising bell being the first sound of which she was conscious. Of her room-mates, Ruth and Eileen were the earliest out of bed, for Pen heard them moving about soon after the bell had sounded. Judy and Dora tumbled out at the last minute and had a great scramble to be ready in time for eight o'clock breakfast.

After prayers and before school there was half an hour which the girls spent in their rooms, making their beds and generally tidying up. Later Pen discovered that it was supposed to be a " quiet time ", although no one would have guessed it from the noise that went on in number eight room!

Pen did not do much on her first day at school. Having arrived on a Thursday she would not begin to work properly until Monday; but she was given text-books and note-books, and was making some pretence of studying them during afternoon preparation on Friday when a message came for her to go to the Head's study. Asking permission to leave, she went downstairs and discovered that her luggage had arrived.

" I am having it taken up to number eight," Miss Martin said, " but as you will not have enough room for all your belongings there, I shall let you use a chest of drawers in my dressing-room for the things that will not be in everyday use. I hardly think you need go back to preparation. Ask Miss Miles to excuse you and tell her that I said you were to unpack."

Pen was pleased at the prospect of seeing her possessions again, and, returning to the class-room, explained matters to Miss Miles. As she left the room for the second time the eyes of the girls followed her speculatively.

About ten minutes after Pen's departure Judy put up her hand and asked permission to fetch a book from her desk in another class-room. Dora grinned, knowing very well that it was an excuse to go and find out what Pen was doing. Curiosity was one of Judy's failings. Permission having been given, Miss Miles took the opportunity of reminding her that all books necessary should have been gathered before preparation began. Once outside the room, Judy dashed downstairs and pulled a book out of her desk; then made straight for room number eight, regardless of the rule that bedrooms were not to be visited during the afternoon without special leave. She felt fairly safe, however, for Miss Edgar was taking Senior preparation and it was Miss Lawson's afternoon off duty.

Pen had taken everything out of one of her cabin trunks and laid them on the bed; her head was buried in another, when she heard a step and looked up. There was Judy's impudent face peering round the door at her.

" So this is what you're up to, is it?" she asked, perching herself on the bed, " I thought I had better investigate. Where on earth are you going to put all that stuff?"

" Aunt Barbara is going to let me use a chest in her dressing-room," Pen answered.

Judy drew herself up and stared.

" Who?" she inquired coldly.

Pen coloured.

" Miss Martin, I mean. You see I have always called her Aunt Barbara; but, of course, I mustn't do it in school."

" I should jolly well think not—" began Judy, suddenly gliding behind the screens which were standing near by. The next moment Miss Martin entered the room.

"I see that you have made great progress with your unpacking," she remarked, surveying the piles of things on the bed. "What a number of books! Are any of them prizes? Let me see, yes, I can give you a small bookcase for them which you may put beside your things downstairs."

Pen murmured her thanks, feeling all the time most uncomfortable on Judy's account, for she guessed that if she were discovered there would be trouble, and, in spite of her unfriendly attitude, she felt oddly drawn to this niece of Miss Martin's.

The Head seemed in no hurry to leave; she sat down on the chair by the bed and picked up a double photograph frame.

"What splendid likenesses!" she exclaimed; "especially the one of your mother. Are you going to set them up on that shelf beside the bed? That is where most of the girls put their photographs. And you are allowed to hang small pictures on the wall beside you; we had that low picture rail put there for that purpose. Have you any school groups?"

Pen answered all these questions as naturally as she could, wishing all the time that Miss Martin would go. Judy, in her hiding-place, was fuming at her capture and wondering what those

in the class-room would be thinking about her
long absence, and especially what explanation
she could give to Miss Miles when she made her
escape, if ever she did! It was all very well to
give her the nickname of " Smiles ". She didn't
always live up to it. After what seemed an inter-
minable time to both girls, Miss Martin rose, and,
saying that Mrs. Philips might be along at any
moment with the man to put up the rails for Pen's
cubicle curtains, she left the room. At once Judy
reappeared.

" Goodness," she muttered, " I thought she
never was going. I wonder whether it's safe
now."

Opening the door softly she peeped out, but
immediately withdrew her head and turned with
a scared face to Pen.

" She's coming back and the others are with
her; whatever shall I do?"

Pen quickly opened her empty trunk, lifted
out the tray and motioned to Judy to get inside.
She had just pulled down the lid when the door
opened to admit Miss Martin, Mrs. Philips and
a workman carrying a pair of steps and a bag of
tools. They stood discussing matters for a
minute; then the Head left and Mrs. Philips
spoke to Pen.

" I don't think that the putting up of the rail
need interfere with your unpacking," she said, at

the same time glancing at the man for confirmation.

" No, that's all right, missis," he answered, " but I'll just move that there box, if yer don't mind," and before Pen could stop him he had grasped the trunk with Judy inside and pushed it behind the bed.

" 'Ope I 'aven't done no 'arm," he inquired as he straightened his back. " Seemed as if something moved w'en I shifted it."

" Oh no, it's quite all right," declared Pen hurriedly, and breathed a sigh of relief when Mrs. Philips went off, saying she would be back later. The workman started on his job, and Pen lifted the lid of the trunk. Judy crept out and tiptoed to the door. A sudden bang made both girls jump, and looking round they saw the man on the top of the steps gazing at them with his mouth open. On the floor was the tool which had slipped from his grasp.

" Just let me know, mate, w'en the next trick is doo," he remarked, wiping his face with a large coloured handkerchief. " It fair gave me a start, that one did ! "

Both girls laughed, and Judy made her escape.

It was not until later that Pen heard the end of the adventure. Judy was furious about it.

" We never used to be given lines to learn," she declared. " It's only since Gracie came that they have become so popular; but why the others follow her example, I can't think. Smiles simply handed them out to me without turning a hair. And if she had known where I had been all the time she would have reported me to Aunt Bee as well."

" Is Miss Lawson a new mistress?" inquired Pen of Dora.

" Gracie? Yes, she only came this term, and Judy has had lines to learn for her five times already."

Judy's voice broke in with:

" I don't believe Aunt Bee knows that she has introduced learning lines as a punishment. I'm sure she wouldn't approve of it."

" You had better tell her, Judy," teased Ruth.

Judy made a grimace.

" There's no good asking for more trouble, is there?" she retorted, " but Gracie has had her knife into me ever since she came, and I'll pay her back one of these days, you see."

" How I wish I had been there when you got into the trunk!" gurgled Dora. " It was jolly clever of you to think of it, Pen. Do tell us about the workman again, Judy. It was screaming."

Judy was not to be drawn, and Pen, becoming aware of her unfriendly attitude, did not comply with the request either.

Miss Martin's dressing-room was an attractive-looking little place, sometimes used as an extra sick room if occasion required, and when Pen had arranged her books on the shelves she felt that the room almost belonged to her. Just before supper she went down to the Head's drawing-room and knocked at the door.

" It's me, Aunt Barbara," she said, on hearing permission to go in. " May I ask you something?"

" Yes, certainly, come along over to the fire," replied Miss Martin. " Have you finished unpacking?"

" Yes, I've got all my things put away, and I wanted to know when the next mail goes to China."

Then she caught sight of Judy over by the window, hunting through the books in one of the bookcases there. She turned her head, and Pen was astonished to see real hostility staring at her from those blue eyes. She had hoped the adventure with the trunk would make them friends, but it seemed far otherwise. Miss Martin picked up *The Times* to look at the outgoing mails, and Pen felt a nose being rubbed against her leg. It was Prince.

" Come here at once, Prince!" Judy commanded, and the dog retraced his steps, only to return to Pen after a few moments.

Miss Martin looked up.

" Prince has taken Pen to his heart, Judy," she

said. "He seems to know that she is specially interested in everything from China."

Judy made no comment but turned back to her search, her thoughts in a turmoil. What right had this new girl to come knocking at Aunt Bee's door and calling her "Aunt Barbara?" That had always been her special privilege and no one else's. Furthermore, Prince seemed to have transferred his allegiance to this newcomer. It really was too bad; he had always been her pet. Jealousy ran through Judy's veins like a fire. Her aunt's voice broke in on her reverie.

"There is a mail out on Monday, I see, Pen, so that should give you plenty of time to write your letter. I shall get one off to your mother by that same mail; she will have received our cable by this time, I hope. Judy," she continued, "did you know that Pen was an adopted niece? She called me 'Aunt Barbara' since she was quite small. You two girls should be good friends."

Judy muttered something. At that moment the supper bell rang, and Pen, at any rate, was very glad.

Chapter 4

AT LOGGERHEADS

THERE was no doubt in the minds of the occupants of number eight room that Judy was very jealous of Pen. It was a side of her character little known to them, for until now she had never shown jealousy of any one.

But then, of course, there had been no cause, for she held a special place in the school, and although Miss Martin was most careful not to show any favouritism—rather the reverse according to Judy—she was the Head's niece and there was no getting away from the fact. Indeed, Judy's airy references to "Aunt Bee" were a continual reminder. Yet the girls did not understand why she should be so jealous of the new girl, and why she should be so delighted to snub or tease her whenever she got the chance.

They liked Pen. She was not conceited or stuck-up. Actually, she was very friendly. They enjoyed asking her questions about China, and nothing pleased them better than when she brought out her Chinese pen and ink, to address her home letter in those peculiar characters all down one side of the envelope. She also let them try their hand at it, and this only increased their wonder that she was able to write such complicated script. Pen did not understand Judy's attitude to her either; but she was very conscious of it, for it was the one thing that prevented her from settling down happily at The Elms, and it made her long desperately for Nan.

The school was looking forward to two important events: a paper chase, which was to take place soon after the half-term, and the water gala, fixed for the last Saturday before school broke up for the summer holidays. The gala was an inter-school affair, the competitors being the several schools in Redheath who went to the baths. As Pen listened to the girls discussing their chances of success in these two events, she gathered that Judy, although a junior, was the school champion in swimming and diving. Actually, she seemed to be the best all-round athlete they had.

Pen was looking forward greatly to taking part in the paper-chase, as it would be a novel experience for her, such things not having been possible at Wu-lu. Much to her disgust, Miss Martin had not, so far, allowed her to go to the baths with the school, because she had developed a tiresome cold soon after arrival in England; but now it had almost gone and she was counting the days until she was allowed to join the others in this part of their recreation. Being very keen on swimming she wondered how the fresh-water baths would compare with that lovely sweep of sea at Wu-lu. Not very favourably, she feared. Then how many lengths would one have to swim to make up a mile, she wondered. Judy had inquired whether she had ever been to swimming baths, and, on hearing that she had always bathed in the sea at Wu-lu, had remarked very scathingly:

"The sea! Any one can bob up and down in the sea."

Pen had made no rejoinder, as she did not want to argue with Judy, and that was what so often she found herself doing, for there was nothing that Judy liked better than to tease Pen about the Chinese. She found she could always arouse her on that subject.

Most of the juniors were sitting round the table at their end of the recreation-room making " scent " for the paper chase. Instead of tearing up old papers and copy books as they had done formerly, they were cutting up lengths of coloured wool so as not to litter the country-side with unsightly paper. Judy was in a bad temper on account of some trouble she had been in with Miss Lawson, and she sought to work it off by

teasing Pen.   She referred to the Chinese as
" Chinks ".

Pen rose to the bait.

" I do wish you wouldn't call them that," she
objected, " it's so rude."

Judy laughed.

" I may call them what I please, I suppose," she
retorted.   "A friend of ours who was an engineer
on a ship that went to China always called them
that, and he knew all about them."   Then she
added provocatively: " He said he once had a
Christian cook who stole a clock from him."

" How did he know that he was a Christian?"
questioned Pen quickly.

" Well, he spoke English," replied Judy airily.

" That doesn't prove he was a Christian,"
returned Pen.   " Lots of Chinese know some
English, but it doesn't make them Christians.   If
he had been a real one he would never have
done a thing like that.   Some of my best friends
are Chinese and they are as good as or better
than—than any of us," and she stammered in her
eagerness to stick up for her friends.

" Speak for yourself, please," replied Judy
coldly.   " I don't particularly like to be compared
with your Chink friends.   Or perhaps," she added
suspiciously, " you don't consider that I am a
Christian."

Pen was silent: she was sorry that the conversation had taken this turn, but Judy was in a belligerent mood.

"I suppose you *do* consider me a Christian," she repeated.

"I don't know whether you are or not," Pen said in a quiet voice.

Judy glared at her.

"You call yourself one, I suppose?" she demanded.

Pen flushed.

"Yes, since some meetings we had at school last term," she replied.

"I see, and you think we are all heathen. I knew you would; I told the others so when we first heard you were coming. But let me tell you that *we* have been born and brought up Christians, having lived in a civilized and Christian country all our days."

Judy was rather pleased with this effort. Pen said nothing for a minute, then remarked quietly;

"Being born in a Christian country doesn't necessarily make anyone a Christian."

Judy stared at her in surprise.

"Whatever do you mean?" she demanded.

"I mean that you have to become a Christian," Pen said. "You aren't born one."

Judy was about to make some rejoinder when the door opened and Maida put her head round the corner.

" Is Pen there? she asked. " Oh, there you are! Would you mind coming and helping me with this address?"

Pen rose and followed Maida out of the room. As the door closed behind them Judy burst out with:

" Isn't she intolerable?"

" You shouldn't tease her so much," protested Eileen. " You know how much she loves the Chinese; it's a shame."

" It isn't only that, it's everything," retorted Judy. " I thought she would be a prig, and now we know she is; setting herself up as being better than any of us, if you please!"

" She didn't do that exactly," objected Dora. " She only answered your question."

Judy ignored this unpalatable reminder and continued her indictment of Pen.

" Look how she toadies to Maida! It's sickening, and in a new girl preposterous."

She glanced round the group of girls as if challenging any one to deny this statement.

Eileen took up Pen's defence.

" I don't think she toadies to Maida," she said. " It's only because Maida's father has gone to Shanghai and Maida wants to know about the place and get some help in addressing her letters."

" Ugh!" grunted Judy, " you don't need to put any Chinese on a letter going to such a well-

known place as Shanghai, and besides, it makes
Pen think she is far more important in the school
than she is. We all got on very nicely before she
came. Then look at the way even Aunt Bee kow-
tows to her."

Here there was a chorus of dissent.

"Miss Martin kow-tows to her! Oh no, Judy,
whatever do you mean?"

"Well, didn't she stop this very morning when
she was reading that article from *The Times,* to
ask Pen how to pronounce some silly old name?"

"But that was only natural," replied Eileen.
"You know how particular the Head is always to
be correct, and those Chinese names are such
tongue-twisters."

"All right, stick up for her if you like," retorted
Judy, and stuffed a pile of cut wool into the bag
she was filling.

Pen rejoined them in a minute or two and they
all worked in silence. Then Judy returned to the
attack.

"I'm so sorry for Maida," she remarked plain-
tively, "having her father in that awful country;
she will be so anxious about him."

The girls murmured their assent, but were not
sure what this remark was leading to, and it did
not satisfy Judy.

"Aren't you sorry for her, Pen?" she inquired.

"Yes, she's bound to be anxious, although I

don't think she need worry too much. It isn't as
if he would be actually fighting."

"How do you know?" countered Judy. "You
don't know very much about it, do you? Anyway
he wouldn't run away like—like some other people
I could mention."

Pen said nothing. Then someone asked:
"Who do you mean, Judy?"

"Oh! civilians and others," she replied. "And
missionaries," she added casually.

This was more than Pen could stand. She
thought of her mother and father and many of
their friends at their posts in the war-stricken
areas, and of those doing refugee and medical
work. Her eyes blazed, and she answered hotly:

"I may not know much about Mr. Jackson, but
you evidently know nothing about missionaries,
and I think you are horribly mean."

Then she rose hastily and left the room.

As she went out of the door she heard Judy
say with a laugh:

"She's got a temper, hasn't she? Even if she
is a Christian."

The girls were collecting the full bags of
"scent" and were about to turn to other things
when the door opened and Pen reappeared. She
looked rather white; but going straight over to
where Judy was still sitting at the table she said,
"I'm sorry I lost my temper just now," and as

Judy was too much astonished to make any reply, she sat down and began to write a letter:

DEAREST NAN (she wrote),

  How I wish you were here! I feel so lost without you, although Aunt Barbara is a dear and the girls quite nice. You remember the one I told you about in my last letter, Judy Martin, a niece of Aunt Barbara's, the girl I feel most drawn to? Well, unfortunately, she doesn't like me at all, and we are always arguing about things, especially Chinese things! And now to-day I have gone and disgraced myself by losing my temper. We were quite right when we thought it wouldn't be as easy to be Christians at home as it was at Wu-lu. I have been thinking about the words of that chorus we used to sing. "No never alone, no never alone, He promised never to leave me, never to leave me alone." But it was I that failed Him to-day. You ask whether I'm on for going to a schoolgirls' camp for a fortnight in August. Rather! And as soon as you send the folder about it, I'll show it to Aunt Barbara. I'm glad you like the High School and Jean sounds very nice; I'll meet her if she is going to the camp. I wish Judy would come, too, because she really is jolly and good at all games, so would enjoy that part of it and might come to like the other too. . . .

It was a long letter, for Pen found there was so much to tell and she had so many questions to ask Nan.

On Wednesday the school went to the baths, and Pen enjoyed herself immensely. She wanted badly to dive off the high board, but those who were to compete in the water gala took possession of that end completely, which perhaps was natural enough. Then Pen conceived a plan. When the whistle went for them all to come out of the water, she would leave with the rest, go to her dressing-box, which she occupied alone; wait a few minutes until all would be busy dressing, then slip out and take just one dive. She really must have one.

Her scheme worked splendidly, even Miss Edgar, who was in charge, being nowhere to be seen. Pen slipped out of the box, which happened, fortunately for herself, to be at the end of the line, and climbed up to the highest board. There was a slight splash as she cut the water like a knife and came up at the shallow end. As she climbed out of the bath she was rather abashed to see the instructor talking to a woman. The woman happened to be a mistress of another school; but Pen, of course, did not know this. As she disappeared into her box the instructor spoke to his companion:

" What girl is that?" She doesn't belong to

The Elms, as far as I know. Is she one of yours?"

" She is not, and I am relieved to hear that she is not one of Miss Martin's pupils, either. If she had been entered for the diving competition in the gala, none of my girls would have stood a chance."

Pen had been seen by someone else. Dora, sharing a box with Judy, happened to put her head out from behind the curtain just as Pen was poised for diving.

" Goodness! " she gasped. Then she held her breath until Pen was in the water.

" What's up?" inquired Judy.

" It's Pen; she's just made a topping dive from the highest board."

" Never!" cried Judy. " It can't have been Pen."

" It was, look! She's coming out."

Judy couldn't doubt the evidence of her eyes, and her words about bobbing up and down in the sea rose to her mind.

" Don't say anything about it, if she doesn't," she commanded and Dora, jumping at once to what was in Judy's mind, agreed.

On the way home Judy's thoughts were not as pleasant as they might have been. Up to this time she had been the school's champion in most diving contests, and now it seemed that her supremacy might be challenged. This was rather serious as matters stood, for Miss Martin had been talking to her about the standard of her work and her conduct generally, and had even hinted that if things did not improve she might not be allowed to take part in the gala. Judy admitted to being a little scared, but had consoled herself with the knowledge that she was the best diver The Elms had, anyway among the juniors, and that Aunt Bee would never let the school down by punishing her in that way. Now, here was Pen, figuring as a champion diver! She could easily take her place. Oh, bother! Was Pen to spoil everything? No, she should not; she would fight her all along the way.

Chapter 5

THE PAPER-CHASE

THE girls in the Fourth were in a lively mood. The slightest thing started them off laughing, so that when Miss Lawson appeared in the place of Miss Martin to take their Scripture lesson it was inevitable that trouble should arise.

"Oh help," murmured Judy, as she came into the room.

Before beginning the lesson Miss Lawson explained to the girls that Miss Martin had been detained by a visitor and had asked her to take this period. Now the Head always made this hour one of the most interesting, and all the girls liked it. They were studying Old Testament history, the time of the Exile, and she had given them many interesting facts about the places mentioned; but it was scarcely fair to expect Miss Lawson to do the same.

After the lesson had been proceeding for some time Judy put up her hand.

"Well?" asked Miss Lawson.

"Miss Martin was beginning to describe to us

the famous Hanging Gardens of Babylon," she said. " Please will you tell us about them?"

Miss Lawson looked a little embarrassed.

" I think we will allow Miss Martin to finish the description herself," she answered.

" Oh, Miss Lawson," pleaded Judy, " do just tell us how they were hung; by ropes, or what?"

One of the girls tittered.

" Well, most things are hung by ropes, aren't they?" retorted Judy. " Pulleys and—and people," she added.

This time the whole class tittered.

" That will do, Judy," Miss Lawson said.

" What? The ropes?" inquired Judy in a low tone which did not carry as far as the desk. Then, speaking louder, she began again.

" Yes, but Miss Lawson, if you can't, I mean if you won't tell us about the Hanging Gardens, do tell us whether it was four-horse chariots that could pass on the walls, or only two."

" I am not going to answer any questions just now." Miss Lawson was a little flushed, and quite conscious that Judy was trying to expose her ignorance.

Judy smiled to herself and scribbled something on a scrap of paper, passing it along to Dora.

When Dora read, " No, because you don't know the answers," she tittered again.

Miss Lawson looked up and demanded of Judy what she was doing.

"Me?" queried Judy in a tone of injured innocence. "Oh, I mean I," she added, whereupon all the girls laughed.

Miss Lawson glared at them from her desk.

"I cannot think what has come over you this morning," she said. "You are not in a fit state of mind for this lesson. I shall tell Miss Martin that I was unable to take it owing to your misbehaviour. Open your Bibles now at the Psalms, and each one of you learn a Psalm by heart, and come and repeat it to me before the day is over. I put you on your honour not to choose one you already know."

The girls, a little abashed by this summary sentence, did as they were bid.

"Which one are you going to learn, Pen?" whispered Eileen from the next desk.

"The 117th," replied Pen promptly.

Eileen turned over the pages of the Bible, found the Psalm, and chuckled behind her handkerchief.

Judy, sitting next to her, looked round.

"What's up?" she whispered.

"No talking!" commanded Miss Lawson.

Eileen, pointing to the open book in front of her, wrote 117 in large figures on a corner of her note-book, edging it to the side of the desk so that

Judy could see it. She nodded her head, and looked up the Psalm. Then her eyes danced. This was too good a suggestion to ignore, even if it had come from Pen. She passed on the information and it went round the class. Silence reigned for some time, the girls keeping their eyes fixed on their books. Then the door opened and Miss Martin entered the room. The class received an unpleasant shock.

" I am afraid that I have come too late to be of much service, Miss Lawson," she said. " You will be nearly at the end of the lesson."

Miss Lawson, looking a little embarrassed, replied:

" I am very sorry, Miss Martin; but I have found it impossible to teach this class on account of its hilarity. The girls are now learning a Psalm as a punishment lesson."

Miss Martin frowned almost involuntarily. She had a strong objection to setting any part of the Bible as a punishment lesson.

" I am very sorry indeed to hear that," she answered gravely. " Thank you, Miss Lawson, for coming to my help; I need not detain you any longer."

The silence could almost be felt when the door closed behind the retiring mistress, and Miss Martin faced the class.

" I am very much surprised to hear such a

report of your conduct, girls," she began. " I am not going to inquire what it was that so upset Miss Lawson that she felt herself unable to take the lesson, or who was mainly responsible. Miss Lawson may report such things to me later; I do not know. But girls of your age should surely be aware that, apart from anything else, it is unkind and impertinent to behave like this to a mistress."

When she had finished her lecture the girls felt very small. This was a side of Miss Martin that Pen had not seen before, and was suitably impressed.

" Have any of you memorized your lines?" the Head inquired some minutes later.

This was more than the girls had bargained for, and they looked at one another in dismay. It was one thing to take a risk with Gracie, quite another with Miss Martin.

As nobody answered her question the Head spoke again.

" Do you know yours, Pen?"

" Yes, Miss Martin," Pen answered reluctantly.

" Then come and repeat them."

Pen rose and went over to the desk, handing her Bible to the Head.

" Which Psalm is it?"

" The 117th."

The class held its breath.

" The 117th, did you say?" asked Miss Martin, looking up.

" Yes," murmured Pen, and repeated the two short verses that comprise the shortest of all the Psalms. The Head handed back the book to her without any comment.

" Eileen, are you prepared?"

" Yes, Miss Martin."

" Then come here."

Eileen obeyed, and standing at the desk passed her Bible across.

" Which Psalm?" came the question.

" The 117th."

They were all called in turn, and one after the other they all repeated the two short verses. When the last girl returned to her seat, Miss Martin said:

" It is superfluous to inquire whether Miss Lawson indicated which Psalm she wished you to memorize, but I shall be interested to know whose choice it was."

There was silence for a moment, then Pen spoke.

" I chose it," she said.

At this moment the bell rang for break, and although the Head looked as if she were going to say something more, she suddenly turned her back on the class and walked to the window, indicating that it was dismissed. The girls filed out of the room, and when the last had disappeared Miss Martin returned to the desk and sat down, her shoulders shaking. "Oh, Pen, you monkey!" she murmured.

Safe in the refuge of the recreation-room the girls burst out laughing.

"Crumbs, what a joke!" cried Dora, "although it didn't feel like one a minute ago. Who would have thought the Head would ask to hear our lines?"

Pen found herself the centre of an admiring group.

"You're a darling," cried Ruth. "What a lot of trouble you saved us! I'm only sorry not to have seen Gracie's face when she discovered our choice of a Psalm."

"Do you think you will get into a row over it, Pen; or all of us for that matter?" asked Eileen.

Judy, who had fully appreciated the situation in the class-room, now felt her jealousy of Pen rising, and she said sharply:

"Gracie put us on our honour not to choose a Psalm we already knew."

"Well," asked Eileen, "did you know the 117th?"

"No, of course not, but it was funny that Pen was able to hit on it at once, wasn't it?"

There was silence, and then Pen spoke.

"I knew about it because I happen to be read-

ing the 119th in the Scripture Union readings,"
she said; " and I noticed what a short Psalm the
117th was."

*Why does Judy always spoil everything?
What makes her hate me so?* Pen asked herself
miserably as she turned away.

"You are a mean thing, Judy!" declared
Eileen indignantly.

" Think so?" retorted Judy carelessly. But she
felt mean. "Anyway, I hope Gracie won't go
and give a detailed account of the Scripture hour;
I don't want to get into any more rows until the
water gala is safely over."

"That's too much to hope for," teased Dora.
" It's not until nearly the end of the term."

Judy ignored this remark and continued:

"Who would have thought a few innocent
questions from an inquiring mind would have
upset Gracie so much. Or any of you, if it comes
to that," she added.

The girls laughed.

"An inquiring mind! That's a good one!"
jeered Dora.

Having once more become the centre of attrac-
tion, Judy regained her good temper.

The day passed without Miss Martin referring
in any way to the happenings of the morning, so,
encouraged by this, Judy told her friends that she
was going to Miss Lawson's study to tell her that

the Head had heard their lines.

"I want to make her ask me to repeat them again," she explained, "just to see her face."

She was not to have that satisfaction, for, on arriving at the study door, she found an "Engaged" notice pinned there, so of course she did not venture to knock. Still, thinking this too good a chance to miss of getting some of her own back, she took a pencil from her pocket and printed underneath, TO WHOM? There was so much merriment caused by the recital of this exploit that Maida pushed open the dividing doors in the recreation-room and inquired whether it was a joke that could be shared. If so, they would like to hear it and then get a little peace and quiet. This made them settle down for fear of further questioning.

"The best of it is that Gracie can't do anything about it," declared Judy, "let alone report it to Aunt Bee; it's not a thing she will want to advertise."

"She will suspect you," remarked Eileen.

"Suspicion never does anyone much harm," replied Judy.

She was to remember these words later.

Saturday, the day of the paper-chase, dawned fine and sunny, and everyone was in good spirits. Maida and Mabel Smith had been chosen as hares, the rest forming the pack of hounds. For the past three years the hares had got safely home, and this year there were many who determined that it was not going to happen again. Judy was of their number, and she reckoned that she had a fairly good chance of catching them, because Mabel was not a champion runner. On the other hand, Maida was a champion at laying false trails!

At 2 p.m. prompt the hares were released with their bags of scent, and ten minutes later the hounds gave tongue. The pack started off at a smart trot, led by some of the bigger girls, Pen keeping beside the members of number eight room. At first the scent was easy to pick up and the pace good. Before long, however, some began to show signs of straggling, and those who were the better runners drew ahead of the others. The course, which had been fixed in consultation between the Staff and the hares, was a run of four or five miles. Up hill and down dale the hounds followed the trail.

" This wool isn't nearly as easy to see as paper," declared Judy, stopping for a moment to regain her breath at the top of an incline. " But come on, we'll pass the leaders in a moment."

And so they did.

" Judy is determined to be among the first home, even if she doesn't catch a hare," laughed Nessie White, as the five girls passed her and three other seniors. " And she is carrying room number eight along with her."

" Don't worry, they can't keep that pace up," replied another senior. " We'll overtake them later. But I admit they are doing rather well."

So Miss Miles thought when they passed her a few minutes afterwards.

" Good!" she said to them. " You are the first. This is a quarter of the run. Keep it up!"

Soon after this, Ruth and Dora developed stitches, and Pen found herself running with Judy and Eileen. Then they came to a place where the trail divided and Judy switched off to the left.

" Are you sure we're all right?" questioned Eileen.

Judy was sure, so they ran on until they came to Tilit Wood. Here the scent was difficult to find and it seemed to be scarcer. Then they lost it altogether and, while searching around, Eileen tripped over the stump of a tree and, pitching forward, fell, cutting her shin on a piece of broken bottle.

" I'm done for," she groaned.

" What a shame to leave old bottles about like that!" cried Judy indignantly.

" You two go on," Eileen said after a minute; " I'll be all right."

Judy frowned and hesitated, and Pen began tying her handkerchief and Eileen's together to make a bandage long enough to meet round the injured leg.

"Yes, you go on," she agreed. "It's no use both of us losing time; but lend me your hankie first to use as a pad. Then I'll help Eileen back to Miss Miles."

Judy complied with Pen's request and, arguing to herself that she really stood a better chance of making home than Pen did, left them and followed the trail out of the wood.

"Looks like a good run here," she said to herself as she surveyed the road making its way down hill, and she set off at full speed. She had gone some distance when, turning round a bend, she suddenly pulled up. In front of her, to her right, gleamed a small sheet of water.

"Bother! I must be wrong," she muttered. "That is the Deadly Pond."

This pond was given that name by the girls on account of the treacherous character of the ground round it, and was strictly out of bounds. She glanced at the road. There was no scent to be seen. In her eagerness to make up for lost time she had lost the trail! Bother Maida, why was she so good at laying traps? Perhaps they had taken the wrong direction at the place where the trail divided. It was funny that none of the others were in sight. If she had to go back she would lose all chance of catching the hares or of getting home first, and would most likely be last!

What worried her more than anything was the thought that perhaps Pen, on going back to Miss Miles, would be set on the right trail and come in before her. Was Pen going to outstrip her in all directions? Then a thought came to her. If she cut across the foot of the pond, this would save her a great deal of time, because it would bring her out fairly near the other road which had borne off to the right. Against rules? Yes, she knew that; but she had once crossed the bog without coming to any harm, so why not again, when so much depended on it? Even while she was debating these matters with herself her steps were taking her in that direction.

She got half-way across the end, where the grass and rushes gave a false impression of solidity, when one of her shoes was sucked off. In her endeavour to recover it she found herself floundering in the wet boggy ground. The more she struggled to extricate herself the farther in she sank. Then she began to be afraid, for still there was nobody in sight, and if she was really on the wrong trail, then perhaps no one would come that way. Someone might arrive, of course, from the other direction, because she knew there were houses and streets not far off. Suddenly her eyes lighted on the shelter at the side of the pond. A life-belt hung there, and Judy gazed at it fascinated.

Chapter 6

HOUNDS IN TROUBLE

PEN helped Eileen through the wood and out on to the road. Then they began a slow and rather painful walk in the direction they had come.

"It's a shame to spoil your run," declared Eileen in a worried tone. "I could manage by myself, I'm sure."

But she was very glad of the assistance of Pen's arm. They plodded on for a little while, and then came across two seniors sitting by the side of the road.

"Hullo, what's up?" they inquired, and on hearing of the accident, volunteered to help Eileen on to where Miss Miles was, with her first-aid case.

"She'll strap your leg up for you, and then it will be much easier to walk on," they declared. "We're winded and out of the running; but if you want to go on, Pen, leave Eileen to us."

So Pen set off once more. Back into the wood she ran, and out again in the same direction that

Judy had taken. She had not gone very far
down the hill, however, when the scent doubled
back on itself, and she stopped. Wondering
whether she was on the right trail, and where all
the others could be, she turned, and started uphill
again.

Suddenly she stopped. Was that some one
calling? She listened intently. Yes, she heard
quite clearly now the cry of " Help! Help!"
coming from farther down. Running back, and
turning the bend in the road, she saw someone
waving from the pond. She had been told about
the bog, and warned not to go near it, and she
knew also that it was out of bounds, so that on
drawing closer and recognizing Judy she was
greatly astonished.

" I'm stuck fast and can't move," shouted Judy.

Pen looked about her; how could she get her
out? Then she found a piece of ground that
looked fairly firm, and made as if to approach
the captive. Judy exclaimed:

"There's no good coming that way; you'll
only get stuck too. I'm sinking farther and
farther in; I don't see how I am ever to get out."

Pen looked round in despair. There was
nobody in sight on the road. What could she do?
She must help Judy somehow. Then her eye
lighted on the life-belt, and she went over and
took it down from the hook.

" I'll throw this to you, and then try to drag you in by the rope," she called to Judy.

But what a weight it was! Would she be able to throw it? She approached as near as she could. " Now!" she cried. But it did not go far enough, so dragging it back with the rope, she tried again. This time it went farther; but not within Judy's reach. .

" The more I struggle to get out," wailed Judy, " the farther in I go."

" This life-belt is too heavy to be of much use," Pen said. " I'll throw the rope, and you can tie it round your waist. Then I'll try to haul you out."

This gave promise of more success, for Judy caught the rope at the first throw. Then Pen began cautiously to draw as near to her as she could. She saw a stretch of grass that looked quite firm, and thinking that she would have more purchase pulling on the rope from there, made for it. Plop! she had gone knee deep in water!

" Do be careful; you'll get drowned," shouted Judy. " The pond is really dangerous, you know, and that part isn't safe at all. Come back to the edge."

This was easier said than done, but at last Pen managed to struggle back, leaving both shoes behind her! Once more on firm ground, she began to pull on the rope. The only effect it seemed to have was to make Judy yell out.

"I say, stop!" she cried. "I'm being cut in two; I'll have to change the knot in the rope; I tied it in a slip knot and as you pull it gets tighter and tighter. Now, that should be better."

Once more Pen pulled with all her might; but Judy did not move. After a rest, she tried again, but with no better success. Then she shouted to Judy:

"I'm on the same level as you, that's why it is no good. I'll go over where the bank is a bit higher and then try again."

Pen was beginning to feel anxious; and was also feeling the strain of the pulling. Was she strong enough to get Judy out? She made for the bank, and then bent all her energy once more to rescuing the prisoner. Suddenly there was a squelching sound and Judy took a lurch forward.

"I've got my feet unstuck," she cried.

"Oh! good!" panted Pen; "can you get out now?"

But it seemed that she was stuck again. This was terrible; was she going to stick after each step?

Pen exerted all her strength once more; but this time Judy did not move. She must get help from somewhere; she would never get her out otherwise.

"O Lord, help us," she prayed.

Then she called to Judy that she would pull
again. She was bending down, trying to recover
her breath from this vain attempt, when Judy
exclaimed in excitement:

" Someone is coming."

Pen straightened up, and looking round, saw a
man running towards them.

" I will help you to save your friend," he said,
when he reached Pen's side.

Both girls stared at him, for the voice came
from a young man with very dark eyes and
straight black hair, who smiled at them encourag-
ingly, showing a row of perfect white teeth. Pen
knew at once that he was Chinese.

" Oh, thank you," she said. " I can't manage
to pull her out."

The young man wasted no time, but laid hands
on the rope at once.

" Now I pull," he called to Judy.

Pen watched anxiously, and to her great relief
Judy moved forward a little. But then she
stopped.

The young man turned to Pen.

" We mustn't let her stop like that," he said.
" Perhaps if we both pulled she could keep on
moving," and turning to Judy he told her to try
to take more than one step at a time. She
promised she would, and Pen took hold of the rope
also.

"Now!" cried the young man, and they both pulled steadily and long. Judy did her best too, and managed to move three steps forward.

"One more tug and you'll be out," cried Pen. Even as she spoke, she was wondering whether she could possibly pull again. But she braced herself to the task, and sure enough, they hauled Judy out. The young man helped her up the bank, for she was quite stiff with standing so long in the bog.

"Now you must get home at once," he said. "But you can't walk; I'll fetch you a taxi, there are some down at the bottom of this hill; I saw them as I came up." He set off walking quickly.

The girls spoke little while he was away. They were both soaked to the skin, covered with mud, and very tired. Pen was thinking how wonderful it was that her prayer had been answered, and that it should have been a Chinese, of all people, who had been sent to save Judy! Judy's thoughts were in a turmoil. Relief at getting out of the bog, and gratitude to the two who had saved her, were uppermost. She knew that the young man was not English, but had not taken in the fact that he was Chinese; and through her feeling of gratitude to Pen there still ran the old antagonism. Why should it have been Pen, out of all the girls, who had come to her rescue? Another thought persistently stabbed her. Aunt Bee would be very angry with her for breaking the rule which put the pond out of bounds, and even more for trying to cross the bog. As a punishment she would forbid her taking part in the water gala, she felt sure. When this thought obtruded itself, it crowded all others out.

It was not very long before their friend returned with a taxi. The girls told him the address of the school, which he passed on to the driver; and then he jumped in beside him.

Pen lowered the window in front of her.

"We don't know how to thank you," she began. "We would never have managed if you had not come, er, Mr. . . ."

The young man turned round.

"My name is Saw," he replied.

"Why, that's my Chinese surname too," answered Pen, her face brightening.

"You know China?" he asked eagerly.

"I was born there; my mother and father are missionaries." She mentioned the district where they lived. Mr. Saw became quite excited, and knelt on the front seat in order to talk more easily.

"But that is marvellous," he cried; "my home is there too. My father knows Mr. Swanson well; it is through him that my family became Christian."

Then Pen knew who he was. He was the son of a rich home not far from where she had been born! Although she had met most of the family, this son had been in America, first at school and then at college.

"I know your parents and your sisters quite well," she exclaimed.

Mr. Saw it seemed, was studying economics at London University, and was spending the week-end in Broomhill, with a friend who took a great interest in foreign students.

"I think it was God who sent me to help the daughter of my esteemed teacher," he said.

"I'm sure it was," Pen agreed.

Judy all this time was listening spellbound. Was this attractive young man, who knew Pen's people and who spoke such good English, really a Chinese, one of the race she was so fond of abusing? It was certainly amazing.

When the taxi drew up at The Elms, Mr. Saw jumped out with them, and stood, hat in hand, smiling.

"Good-bye," he said.

"Oh! but you must come in and see Aunt Barbara, mustn't he, Judy?" Pen exclaimed.

"Of course; she will want to thank him for what he has done," she replied.

Mr. Saw demurred; but at this moment the door of The Elms opened and Miss Martin appeared.

"My dear girls, what has happened?" she

exclaimed in horror.

It was no wonder that she gazed at them in amazement, for they were truly a sorry sight.

" We got stuck in the bog and couldn't get out; Mr. Saw came to our rescue," explained Judy.

" He knows Mother and Dad, Aunt Barbara," added Pen.

Miss Martin turned to him.

" You must come in and tell me about it, and let me thank you properly," she said cordially. " Never mind your shoes," she added, as she saw him look down at the mud which was caked on them. Then turning to the girls she said:

" It is hot baths and hot drinks and bed for both of you, and at once. Here is Mrs. Philips; she will see that you get off to bed as soon as possible."

Chapter 7

THE SEQUEL

"JUST come up to my sitting-room," Miss
Martin said, turning to Mr. Saw. "I am
anxious to know what happened. I cannot understand the girls being near that pond; there is a
very strict rule forbidding it."

Mr. Saw described how he was taking a walk
on the Common and how, as he neared the pond,
he saw a girl standing on the bank, pulling with
all her might on a rope, which he discovered was
tied round the waist of another girl who was
almost up to her knees in the bog.

"I hurried along to offer my help, for your
niece was nearly exhausted; she had been putting
out all her strength for a long time. My part was
a very small one; I only added my strength to
hers."

"You are too modest," replied Miss Martin.
"The girls would have been in a sorry plight if
you had not gone to their rescue. I am most
grateful and thank you for what you did, not
only on my own account, but on behalf of the

girl's parents. Penelope mentioned that you know her parents. What a wonderful coincidence that you should have been the one to go to her assistance!"

"It is a small thing to have done for the daughter of my teacher," Mr. Saw replied.

After talking for a little while longer, he rose to leave.

"I am happy to meet a sister of Mrs. Swanson," he said, bowing over her hand.

"Oh, but I am not a sister, only a friend," corrected Miss Martin.

"But Miss Swanson—she called you aunt," began Mr. Saw. Before Miss Martin could explain matters to him, Miss Edgar appeared, evidently wishing to speak to the Head, so he departed, saying that he would call the following day to inquire for the young ladies. On his way home he was thinking that he had mastered these English relationships. Pen Swanson had certainly called Miss Martin "aunt". If she were not a sister of Mrs. Swanson's, how could that be? He gave it up.

After he had left, Miss Martin turned to Miss Edgar. "A most interesting man," she said. "and one to whom we owe a great debt. I shudder to think what might have happened if he had not seen the girls in their distress and gone to their help. Curiously enough, his home is where Pen's parents are at work, so he knows them."

"How very strange!" commented Miss Edgar. "I came to tell you that Mrs. Philips says that Pen has a temperature, and she wants to know whether she should put her into the sick-room, rather than up in room eight."

"Certainly," replied Miss Martin, "it would be much the wisest thing to do. I hope the child is not going to be ill; both of them will have contracted colds, I am afraid. Perhaps it would be just as well, in the circumstances, to keep Judy out of room eight also; she can go into the dressing-room. I am much disturbed over this affair. From what Mr. Saw told me Pen must have tried to cross the boggy end of the pond, and Judy must have gone to her rescue."

"I know that the course we fixed on did not go near the pond," said Miss Edgar, "but some of the girls followed a false trail."

"You might send Maida to me, I would like to question her about it," Miss Martin replied.

"I just wanted to ask you about the run this afternoon, Maida," she said later, when the head girl appeared at her study. "Did you keep to the route agreed on?"

"Yes, Miss Martin, it wasn't altered in any way."

"Then there was no scent laid down by the pond?"

"No, but we laid a false trail in that direction, doubling back past Tilit Wood."

"Did many of the girls follow that false trail?"

"One or two did, but they gave the chase up when they found they had gone so far out of the way."

"They all know the rule about the pond, do they not?" continued Miss Martin, "Pen as well as the others?"

"Yes, they all know the rule, that was why we thought when they found themselves bearing in the direction of the pond, that they would know they were on a false trail," Maida asserted.

"Well, it might have been worse than it has turned out to be," Miss Martin said. And she told Maida how Mr. Saw had described to her what he had seen. "We shall hear the story from the girls themselves, later; but I do not wish to question them to-night. I feel too thankful for their safety to be angry with Pen, although if she deliberately broke the rule, she must be punished."

Neither Pen nor Judy passed a comfortable night. Pen coughed a lot, and Judy developed a heavy cold in the head. Furthermore, Pen's temperature remained up, so in the morning Miss Martin telephoned for the school doctor, Dr.

Clerk. Before getting ready for church, Dora tiptoed into the dressing-room.

"Hullo, old thing," she whispered to Judy, "how are you? Maida heard from the Head about your trying to rescue Pen from the Deadly Pond, and we're all jolly proud of you. I mustn't stop though, I'm terrified of being caught. You *have* got a dose of cold, haven't you? So long!" She disappeared as noiselessly as she had come, narrowly missing Miss Martin and Dr. Clerk as they came upstairs.

"Well, young woman," the doctor said, greeting Judy. "Been trying to qualify for the Royal Humane Society's medal, eh? You're a plucky girl. Now don't begin to disown the praise; just keep quiet and let me see what damage has been done. Do you complain of anything special? Streaming nose, sore throat, head like a cabbage? Just what I expected. Pain anywhere? In your legs? Well, that's not to be wondered at; you've got a real dose of cold all through you. But we'll have you all right in a day or two; bed is the place, though, meantime." Rising, he followed Miss Martin out of the room, without giving Judy much chance of opening her mouth. So that was what they all thought—that she had rescued Pen! Well, after Dr. Clerk had seen Pen they would change their tune. Judy fell to brooding over the situation in no happy state of mind.

" So you're the young woman who tried to cross the bog, being finally rescued by a Chinaman, are you?" began Dr. Clerk, as he sat down beside Pen's bed. " Yes, I know all about it, you see," he continued, as Pen raised astonished eyes to his.

" But . . ." she began and then changed to : " Have you seen Judy?"

" Just come from her room; she's got a fine dose of cold for her pains, but you haven't killed her off. Don't worry about her; she will be all right in a day or two."

So Judy had not corrected the story. Why? Pen determined to say nothing until she had time to think things out.

" Feeling pretty tired, aren't you?" inquired the doctor, as he put his stethoscope back into his pocket.

" A little," admitted Pen.

" It was a paper-chase you were bent on, wasn't it? Had you been running hard before you got to the pond?"

" Yes, on some parts of the course."

" A bit short of breath, eh?"

" Oh! no," replied Pen decidedly.

The doctor looked a little incredulous.

" Not used to running much, perhaps?"

" Well, I haven't done a great deal since coming to this country," Pen admitted. " I did quite a lot in Wu-lu."

"Wu-lu!" he repeated. "Where on earth is that?"

Here Miss Martin broke into the conversation.

"Pen has only been a few weeks in this country, doctor," she explained. "She was born and brought up in China."

"Tuts!" he exclaimed. "You people who have lived in the East shouldn't go falling into ponds. You didn't happen to know the man who fished you out, I suppose?"

Once again Miss Martin recounted the strange coincidence.

"Extraordinary!" was his comment. "Well, we must get rid of that cough," he added. I'll see you to-morrow," and shaking hands with Pen he left the room.

"Your niece will be all right when she gets rid of her cold," he began, when he was back in Miss Martin's room. "Keep her quiet though, and give her the medicine I shall send along. I am not so happy over the other girl, Pen, I think you called her. Her cold has gone to her chest, but she has also strained her heart. However, rest is a wonderful thing. I'll make her up a bottle too, and we'll hope neither of them will be long the worse for their adventure."

As the doctor was leaving, Mr. Saw appeared with a curious-looking package tied up in a coloured cloth. In answer to Miss Martin's invitation to come in he shook his head. He had only called to ask for Miss Swanson and her friend, he said, and, carefully untying the knots in his cloth, produced two baskets of fruit.

" I hope they will be allowed to have them?" he said, looking at the doctor. His consent being given, Miss Martin promised to have the gifts sent to the girls at once. She then introduced him to the doctor, and they went down the drive together.

Judy was feeling miserable. It had been taken for granted by everybody, apparently, that Pen was the one who had transgressed the rule, and got stuck in the bog. The most astonishing fact of all was that Pen hadn't contradicted the story! She could not have done that because the Head would have said something about it when she looked in with the fruit after the doctor's visit.

An overwhelming temptation came on her. Why not let them go on thinking this? It wouldn't be telling a lie, because no one had asked her about it; and Pen wouldn't get into nearly so bad a row as she would. She knew only too well what it would mean for herself! So Judy reasoned. Of course, Pen might give the true version of the story at any moment; but would she? If she had been going to do it she would have told Dr. Clerk and Aunt Bee this morning. Then a picture of Pen, wet and bedraggled, standing on the bank above the bog and pulling for all she was worth rose up before Judy's eyes, and she felt suddenly ashamed. Pen would never act a lie as she was now tempted to do. The girl that she had badgered and teased and called a prig; of whom she had been so jealous because every one liked her, was quite above doing a mean thing. Judy turned restlessly in bed; she did wish her head wasn't so stupid and fuzzy. The doctor was quite right in his description of it as like a cabbage!

Then her eyes lighted on the basket of fruit sent to her by Mr. Saw. All the things she had said about "Chinks" rushed into her mind, and her cheeks burned. Not only did she owe him a debt of gratitude for saving her, but now he had put her still further into his debt. Pen, of course, he looked on as an old friend, but he had been under no obligation to include a stranger in his gifts. She recalled the conversation in the taxicab. How pleased he had been to discover that Pen was a daughter of the Swansons, and how proudly he had told her that his family had become Christians through her father's preaching.

"Become Christians"—that phrase again! Why did it always come back and back into her mind? Ever since that day when she had roused Pen by her story of the Chinese boy who had stolen the clock, and was, she asserted, a Christian, those words of Pen's about not being born a Christian, but having to become one, had haunted her. Now, forced to lie in bed with nothing to do but think, it came to Judy suddenly that she had never " become a Christian ". She had taken everything for granted; gone to church on Sundays, read her Prayer Book some mornings; and had even given in her name for attending confirmation classes next term. It was the thing to do, of course, when one reached a certain age. She faced the truth for the first time. Well, anyway, she would confess to Aunt Bee about the bog, and clear Pen; then surely her mind would be more at peace.

Judy was not to get peace of mind so easily, because when her aunt came in to see her later in the day, it was with a worried and anxious look on her face.

" I have just had a telephone call from Southdown," she said. " Your Aunt Maud has had a nasty motor-car accident and they want me to go at once. I shall leave just as soon as I can."

So Judy could not unburden herself, and cause her aunt further worry at such a time.

Before setting out Miss Martin spoke to Miss Edgar, whom she was leaving in charge.

" I'm very sorry to have to desert you like this," she said, " especially with two girls in the doctor's hands. Judy will be up quite soon, I hope, and in regard to Pen, just follow the doctor's orders, and don't hesitate to send for him at any time. I trust I may not be away too long, but I have every confidence in you."

Miss Edgar said she hoped Miss Martin would find her sister's condition not too serious; and assured her that they would manage all right in her absence and that she must not worry over school affairs.

The Head left that evening, and before she returned many things happened at The Elms.

Chapter 8

AT PEACE

THE following evening, in the recreation-room, the juniors were discussing the exciting events of recent days.

"And to think that we all thought it was Judy that went to save Pen, instead of its being the other way round!" exclaimed Eileen.

"Well, seeing we were told it was, we could hardly help thinking it," retorted Dora. "Poor Judy! I wonder what ever made her try to cross that bog; she knew it was dangerous, besides being out of bounds."

"We shan't know why she did it until we are allowed to see her, and it's funny that Miss Martin will still be blaming Pen," put in someone else.

"But Judy has written to her; Eddie said she might after she had confessed to her," asserted Dora. "Judy told me so when I slipped in this morning to see her."

"You'll slip in once too often," cautioned Ruth, "and find yourself caught. Mrs. Philips said we were not to be allowed to visit them until their colds were a bit better."

" Pen is looking very tired," declared Eileen; " I managed to get a glimpse of her through the door to-day."

" I don't wonder," rejoined Ruth; " she must have nearly done for herself in trying to move Judy."

" This will mean no water gala for Judy, I'm afraid," grumbled Dora. " The Head will never let her take part in it now. Judy told me that the next row of any sort would mean that. I can't think what made her risk so much."

"You know Judy always risks things," Eileen said. " But who can take her place in the diving events?"

" Oh, Pen can do that," returned Dora, forgetting for the moment that she had agreed to conceal this fact.

" Pen!" cried Ruth. " How do you know that she can dive?"

Dora recounted what she had seen that day at the baths.

" But Maida said Pen had strained her heart, so perhaps she won't be allowed to take part, either," she added.

" I wonder whether this adventure will make Judy like Pen any better," mused Eileen.

" Not if she steps in and takes her place in the gala," prophesied Dora.

"Well, I hope Miss Martin won't be away long," Eileen remarked, changing the subject. "Everything seems wrong, somehow, when she's not here."

"Talking of things being wrong reminds me that I haven't found my watch yet," declared Dora. "I wish I could remember whether I was wearing it on Saturday or not."

"Where do you keep it when you're not wearing it?" inquired Eileen.

"I generally do wear it; but at night I lay it on the top of the dressing-table—and it certainly isn't there now."

"You must have dropped it off your wrist," Ruth said. "You remember you told us the strap was frayed."

"You're as bad as I am," laughed Eileen. "I never remember where I put things. That little brooch of silver and enamel that I sometimes wear on Sundays has disappeared. I can't find it anywhere."

"I do wish I could go and see Judy," grumbled Dora. "I'm longing to tell her the news about Gracie. I tried this morning, but Smiles met me on the stairs and asked me where I was going."

Miss Lawson had created quite a sensation in the school by appearing with a diamond ring on the third finger of her left hand.

"It's screaming, coming so soon after Judy

wrote that up on her door, isn't it?" laughed Ruth. " I wonder whether she suspects who did that."

" She's sure to think it was Judy," replied Dora. " They all suspect her when anything really interesting happens. I wonder whether she will get married soon."

" Who? Judy?" inquired Ruth.

" No, silly, Gracie."

" Let us hope so," replied Eileen, thus voicing all their minds. Miss Lawson had no supporters in room number eight.

Miss Martin remained away from day to day. Her sister had not regained consciousness, and until that happened she did not wish to leave her. Miss Edgar sent reassuring reports of the school and of the invalids. Judy was to be allowed up, and Pen was improving rapidly. Dr. Clerk had expressed satisfaction at hearing the true account of the adventure, because it gave him a reason for Pen's tired heart.

" You will be quite fit again, when I let you get up," he had said to her, and to Judy's anxious inquiries about Pen, he had made the same reply.

" Will she be able to play games all right and— and swim, and things like that?" Judy had wanted to know.

She would be fit for everything, he had assured her, as long as she did nothing foolish.

Judy had received an answer to her letter confessing about the pond, Miss Martin saying that she was telling Miss Edgar to take no steps about it until she returned.

The day came when Judy was to be allowed to spend the day in the sick-room with Pen. She felt awkward and not at all like her usual assured self, when she saw her schoolmate lying propped up in bed.

" Hullo, Judy," Pen said, " are you better?"

" I'm all right," replied Judy shortly. " How are you?"

" I'm getting on fine. Dr. Clerk says I will soon be quite fit again."

Judy went over to the bed, and then burst out with:

" I'm awfully sorry for everything, Pen. It's my fault that you are lying here; and I never even thanked you for getting me out of the bog."

" Well, I didn't, because it was Mr. Saw."

" Yes, I know; but you did most of the hard work before he came. If you hadn't got me unstuck, he wouldn't have been able to pull me out. And he wasn't able to, even then, without your help."

Once begun, it seemed that Judy had to get everything off her chest. She told Pen exactly what had happened.

" I was jealous of you when I thought you

might get ahead of me; that was the cause of everything. I've been jealous of you ever since you came, because you were an extra pupil, and Aunt Bee had never broken her rule before for any one. And, worst of all, I let them think that you were to blame for this pond business."

"If you had as little chance of speaking as I had, I don't wonder," Pen replied. "Dr. Clerk asks a lot of questions, but he generally answers them himself!" She laughed.

"I was going to tell Aunt Bee the very first chance I had," Judy continued, "but then she heard about the accident, and I didn't like to worry her any more. I told Eddie, of course, and then I wrote to Aunt Bee, so they all know now. I can't think what made them all so certain that it was you who tried to cross the bog. And Pen, why didn't you correct them when you saw they had it all wrong?"

Pen was silent for a moment and then answered in rather an embarrassed voice.

"Well, for one thing I didn't get much chance, as I told you. Then I found that you hadn't corrected the story, and I thought that if I said nothing you would know that I wasn't trying to get you into a row, or trying to curry favour, or anything of that sort."

Then changing the subject quickly, she added:

"I had a letter from Aunt Barbara, too. It

was something Mr. Saw said that led to the mistake.

"Was that it?" exclaimed Judy. "I wonder what he said. And oh, Pen, Mr. Saw has made me feel so ashamed."

She did not need to say why. Pen understood.

Judy had not finished.

"Tell me about the school you were at in China," she said.

Pen looked surprised, but willingly acquiesced. She was always ready to talk on that subject.

"Were they all Christians there?" Judy asked, after hearing Pen's description.

Now what exactly did she mean? Pen hesitated before answering, remembering only too well the last occasion that this subject was touched on.

"We were all British. There were no Chinese pupils, if that is what you mean," she said.

"I didn't mean that," replied Judy, almost crossly. "You said, Pen, that no one was born a Christian, but had to become one, and——"

"Oh!" cried Pen, hastening to her rescue, "I see what you mean. No they weren't, although quite a lot of us became Christians last term, after some special talks we heard from a visitor to the school."

"Became", that word again!

"Well, I am not one," said Judy in a low voice,

" and I don't know how to ' become one ', as you call it."

Pen's heart gave a little leap.

" Do you want to?" she asked.

Judy nodded.

" Mr. Scott who took those meetings, gave us a text from St. John's Gospel," Pen began rather shyly. " It says there: ' But as many as received Him to them He gave power to become the sons of God; even to them that believe on His name '."

" I've always gone to church," Judy said. " Isn't that believing? And, besides, we say the Creed every Sunday, ' I believe. . . .' "

" I think what it means is to believe in Jesus Christ as our Saviour," Pen said.

Judy made no comment, and Pen hurried on.

" Mr. Scott said ' believe ' meant trust; and he taught us a chorus that helped a lot of us. It went like this:

> " Come into my heart, Lord Jesus,
> Come in to-day,
> Come in to stay,
> Come into my heart, Lord Jesus."

At this rather inopportune moment Mary arrived to polish the floor of the sick-room, and Judy moved away from Pen's bed.

Mary was a favourite with all the girls at The Elms, and many a cubicle had she furtively tidied up, thus saving the owner from getting into trouble.

"So you're up, Miss Judy. Number eight room isn't like itself without you," she remarked.

Judy grinned, but spoke with mock severity.

"Now what do you mean by that, Mary?" she demanded. "That they are all going to the dogs without my influence to restrain them?"

"Yes, *I don't think*," replied Mary.

As she took the mop to polish under the bed, she addressed Pen.

"Do you have monkeys in China, miss?" she asked.

"Monkeys? Yes, in some parts," answered Pen in astonishment. "I have seen them in the hills not far from my home."

"Chancy little beasts," returned Mary.

"What do you know about monkeys, Mary?" asked Judy.

Mary smiled to herself, but vouchsafed no answer.

"Come on, out with it," Judy teased, taking hold of the end of the mop.

"Well," Mary said, "Lena's young man—Lena is my friend, and is kitchen-maid next door at Professor Latham's, you know—well, her young man has given her one to keep for him while he is away."

"Given her a monkey!" exclaimed Judy.

Mary nodded.

" But what does Professor Latham say to it?" queried Pen, " or does he like monkeys?"

" Sakes! he don't know anything about it, nor does Cook; only the housemaid knows. Lena keeps it shut up in an old shed and only lets it out at night."

" Poor little thing, what a shame!" cried Judy.

" It won't be for long," Mary assured her. " And, anyway, he's used to being shut up in the daytime and out at night, so his master says."

" What does his master do?" asked Judy.

They were not to know what he did, for Mrs. Philips came into the room and Mary returned with great vigour to her polishing.

That evening Dora and Eileen were given permission to visit the sick-room, and after hearing from the two invalids a vivid description of their adventure in the bog, they entertained them with lively chatter about school affairs.

" Isn't it priceless about Gracie?" laughed Dora.

They agreed that it was.

" I haven't seen the ring," Pen said. " She hasn't been in since she got it, or if she has, she hadn't it on. They have all been awfully decent in coming to see me—Miss Miles and Miss Lawson as well as Miss Edgar."

" I must congratulate Gracie when I see her,"

said Judy solemnly.

There was a shout of laughter.

" You would never have the nerve," Eileen declared.

" All right, just you wait and see," retorted Judy. After all, how was she to know the way events were shaping?

The next morning after the doctor's visit, Judy was again allowed to spend the day with Pen. She had almost got over the effects of her chill, and was expecting any day to be sent back to school.

She greeted Pen with:

" I've done it."

Pen knew what she meant at once. Had she not been praying that Judy would take the definite step?

" Oh Judy," she exclaimed: " I *am* glad."

" You'll have to help me, Pen; I don't feel a bit different; and you know what I'm like, quick tempered and always doing things on the spur of the moment. My red head has something to do with it, I think," she added ruefully.

" Of course I'll help you," Pen promised, " and you'll help me too; but we haven't got to do it alone. This is what has helped Nan and me a lot," and she quoted:

> " *No, never alone, no, never alone ;*
> *He promised never to leave me,*
> *Never to leave me alone.*"

" I should like to learn some of those choruses,"
Judy said. " Are they in a book?"

" Yes, and I've got a copy; we'll try some of
them over when I get up. You don't know what
it's going to mean to me to have you keen on
these things."

" What a beast I've been to you, Pen," Judy
said vehemently; " but I'm not a bit jealous of
you now. I wonder why I ever was?"

During the next days the girls grew in intimacy.
Judy, of course, had always attracted Pen, and
now they had a strong link holding them
together.

" I'm afraid Nan won't like it, if we become
close friends," Judy remarked one day.

Pen laughed.

" You needn't worry," she said, " Nan's not like
that. And nothing could alter our friendship for
one another, no matter how many new friends
we made. Besides, she has got a chum in Glasgow
now. I'm looking forward to meeting her at the
camp in Fife, if Aunt Barbara will let me go."

" What camp?" asked Judy with interest.

Pen told her all she knew about it, and of the
jolly times spent at different holiday resorts by
schoolgirls from all different parts of the country.

" I'll show you the folder as soon as Nan sends
it," Pen promised, " and perhaps you might care
to come too."

Judy's sick leave was almost at an end. In fact she was to join the classes next day. She was quite fit again.

"I will miss you dreadfully," said Pen, when Judy announced that she was to move her things back to room number eight that afternoon.

"It's a shame that I am well first," declared Judy, "when everything has been my fault, too, but Dr. Clerk said it wouldn't be long now before you were allowed to get up, didn't he?"

"Yes, I am getting better quicker than he thought I would; and to-day he said I might get up for a little this afternoon."

"I shan't feel really happy until Aunt Bee is back and I've got my sentence," Judy said. "Although I know what it will be. But there's a lot of things I must tell her about."

"Well, keep out of trouble now, if you can," Pen answered, "and beware Miss Lawson."

"Right you are; I must keep a watch on my red hair," agreed Judy grinning.

That of course, was just what she did not do.

"It's great to be back," she declared that evening, looking round number eight room. "Solitary confinement would not suit me. And it will be better still when Pen gets back too."

"I thought you felt that she was one too many," exclaimed Dora, "and that you would have had enough of her these days. Have you been badger-

ing her, or letting her down lightly because she
tried to save you?"

Judy flushed. It had to come some time, so
perhaps the sooner the better.

" I've been a beast to Pen," she began, " but
I'm going to make it up to her, if I can. She"s
been a brick, and I believe she would have taken
all the blame about the pond just because she
knew it would mean a big row for me. There
are not many girls who would act in such a
sporting way as that. And I take back all I said
about the Chinese. I didn't know what I was
talking about. There are heaps of them probably
far better Christians than I am."

Here she stopped, hesitated a second, and then
took the plunge.

" I wasn't one at all when I was arguing that
day with Pen. I've only just become one."

The girls looked at one another in astonishment.
This certainly was a new Judy. However, they
rose to the occasion and covered any embarrass-
ment that they felt by joining in her praise of
Pen.

" You're quite right," Eileen said. " Pen is
tophole; and we shall all be glad if you are going
to be friends with her."

They were too shy to refer to the last part of
Judy's confession, but it made a great impression
on them.

"And how have you been getting on without me?" inquired Judy, returning to her usual bantering. "Mary seemed to think that you were rather too sedate and tidy."

"I don't know about being specially tidy," replied Ruth, "but things have been vanishing in a mysterious way."

They told her of various trinkets that they had lost.

"But they can't really have disappeared," objected Judy.

"I'd like to know where they are, then," declared Ruth.

The following afternoon, as Pen was sitting reading, the door opened and Judy entered. There was a mischievous look on her face as she pirouetted round the room, waving her arms about. She drew nearer and nearer to Pen; then passed her left hand in a graceful sweep across her face. Pen was first amused, and then horrified, to see on the third finger of her left hand a flashing diamond ring.

"Judy!" she gasped, laughing in spite of apprehension. "Where did you get it? And, oh! do be careful."

"It's someone else who should be careful," Judy retorted. "Gracie shouldn't leave her property lying about. I found it on the wash-hand basin in the top bath-room."

"It is a beauty," said Pen. "But do go and put it back."

"Right you are! Just thought you might like to see it. There's no harm done," returned Judy.

Then she disappeared as suddenly as she had come.

The next day when the teachers gathered together in their sitting-room after tea, Miss Lawson exclaimed in a worried tone of voice:

"I am afraid I must report the loss of something, Miss Edgar."

"Nothing valuable, I hope?"

"Yes, my engagement ring."

"Oh, surely not," cried Miss Miles. "You must have mislaid it."

"I have searched everywhere for it, and I cannot find it," she replied.

"Have you asked Mary whether she has seen it?" inquired Miss Edgar.

"Yes, I have asked all the maids, and not one of them has."

"I shall mention the loss to the girls to-night," promised Miss Edgar. "It must be somewhere in the school. You could not have lost it outside, could you?"

"No, for I had it yesterday morning, I know; and I have not been out since," Miss Lawson replied.

It was a very subdued-looking Judy who crept

into the sick-room later that evening.

"Pen," said she, "something terrible has happened. Gracie's ring is lost, and Eddie wants to know whether any of us has seen it. What on earth shall I do? I put it back last night just where I found it. You do believe me, don't you?"

"Of course I believe you," Pen declared. "What a dreadful thing to have happened! I'm terribly sorry."

Judy sat down on a chair, the picture of misery.

"I shall have to tell that I saw it at the side of the basin; and if she asks me whether I touched it, then the whole silly thing will come out. What can I do? If it isn't found, Gracie will always suspect me, even if she doesn't say so. Why did I touch the wretched thing? Pen, why should this have happened just after I was going to try to keep out of scrapes?"

Pen tried to comfort her.

"You didn't take it, Judy, so no one can prove that you did. Let's pray about it; He knows where it is and we'll ask Him to help us to find it."

"May we pray for things like that?" asked Judy in surprise.

"Of course, we may pray about everything."

Judy felt a little more cheerful after this, and screwed up her courage to go to Miss Edgar

"It may have slipped down the pipe of the basin," she said hopefully, as she left the room.

She did not feel very brave, however, when she faced Miss Edgar and told her that she had seen the ring.

"In the top bath-room, last night?" repeated Miss Edgar. "Then it should not be very far away. Miss Lawson must have taken it off to wash her hands and forgotten to pick it up again. You didn't touch it, of course?"

Judy flushed and admitted that she had; but declared that she put it back in exactly the same place.

"Then you actually lifted it?"

"Yes, Miss Edgar."

"But that was surely a strange thing to do, Judy. You had better tell me exactly what your movements were."

Thus the whole story had to be told and, in the telling, what had seemed an innocent joke suddenly appeared an unwarranted impertinence. Judy wished she could sink into the ground. Miss Edgar regarded her severely.

"What induced you to act in such an extraordinary way?" she asked. "I could have understood your touching it if you had intended returning it to Miss Lawson, or even just to have a look at it. But what made you act as you did?"

This was just what Judy could not explain.

Had Miss Edgar ever done silly things, suddenly, without thinking?

"There was a possibility that it may have slipped down the waste, as you suggest; we must examine it and also search the bath-room thoroughly." Then, having finished her lecture, Miss Edgar let Judy go.

A search was made that evening, and again the following day; but no ring was found. Judy passed two of the most miserable days in her remembrance.

"Gracie may say that she accepts my word that I put the ring back," she lamented to Pen, "but she half suspects me all the same."

"She can't suspect you of stealing," Pen declared.

"I don't know so much," Judy replied gloomily; "I feel as if everyone did."

She remembered what she had said about suspicion hurting no one, and thought how lightly she had made the assertion, without knowing anything about the matter!

"We'll go on praying," Pen said. "I'm sure everything will come right soon."

Maida visited the sick-room soon after this conversation, and Judy, fancying that she looked coldly at her, rose and left. As they talked together, Maida mentioned that she had lost a clasp, and Pen repeated what Dora and Eileen had said about things going amissing in their room. Maida stared.

"But this is serious," she said. "I must tell Miss Edgar about it at once."

After listening to Maida's story, Miss Edgar puckered her brows.

"It is very worrying," she said. "The girls should have reported it before. Now Mary says two of Miss Martin's Apostle spoons have disappeared. I don't like it at all, and coming on the top of the loss of the ring it is most suspicious. I must get in touch with Miss Martin and tell her about it. I cannot take the responsibility of doing nothing. She may think we should call in the police.

Chapter 9

THE MYSTERIOUS THIEF

PEN sat up in bed, suddenly wide awake. She looked at the clock on the table beside her. It said twelve-thirty. What had awakened her? Then she stiffened and held her breath, while her heart pounded in her side and seemed to be beating in her throat as well, making it difficult to breathe. Someone was in the room. She felt a presence, although it was too dark to see anything. What should she do? Could it be a burglar? She thought of all the things that had been missing from the school, and especially of Miss Lawson's ring. Suppose this was the thief. What *could* she do? He must be caught for every one's sake, but especially for Judy's.

Then Pen received one of the greatest frights of her life, for, as she sat quite still wondering what action to take, the clock beside her suddenly disappeared. It must have been lifted from under her very nose, for she had been staring at its illuminated face and now it was gone! She fought her fear and, reaching up, turned the knob of the switch above the bed.

The room was flooded with light, and she saw the thief with her clock climb on to the window-sill and make his escape through the top of the window.

She lay back in bed shaking, but with a feeling of great relief. It was Lena's monkey! Of course she did not know that he had stolen the other things; but it was a possibility. She made up her mind to tell no one but Judy of the night's adventure, and the two of them would try to discover whether or not the monkey was the culprit. Mary had said that he was only let out at night; well, he made good use of his freedom, it seemed. How thankful she was that Dr. Clerk had given her permission to go out now for a little every day; she must make good use of her freedom too! How wonderful it would be if the mystery were cleared up before Miss Martin returned! This adventure might be the answer to their prayers.

The next morning when Judy came to report her interview with Miss Edgar, Pen poured out her story. Judy was as excited over it as Pen herself.

"How awful for you!" she said, "but how marvellous! Of course that monkey has got all the missing things hidden somewhere. Wouldn't it be wonderful if we found them, and I could present Gracie with her ring?"

"We must think out a plan," Pen said. "You remember that Mary said he was kept in an old shed in the garden, so perhaps he hides his treasures there. We must find that shed, anyhow; that's the first step."

"Let's slip away during tennis this afternoon; it should be quite easy, because they know that I shall be walking up and down the garden with you part of the time," exclaimed Judy. "Oh, bother! There's that bell. I wish I were still on the sick list."

Events turned out as the girls desired, and, after watching the beginning of two sets of tennis, Pen and Judy wandered off together to the end of the garden. There a high wall separated Miss Martin's property from that of Professor Latham.

"We'll need to get over here, and risk making our way back by this gate, I'm afraid," Judy said. "I'll get the ladder which we saw propped against the tool shed; you mustn't risk pulling yourself up on walls yet, Pen."

In turn they mounted the ladder and dropped down into the professor's garden, and were astonished to find themselves in what was almost a wilderness.

"It doesn't look as if he kept a gardener, anyway," Pen remarked, "so that's one thing to the good."

Creeping along by the wall, they made their way towards some sheds which were half hidden by trees. On getting near enough to see them distinctly, they found one was an old greenhouse, and two appeared to be tool sheds. They were all in disrepair. Deciding it was unlikely that the monkey would be kept in the greenhouse, as some of its glass was broken, they moved cautiously towards the first shed.

" I wonder whether we are visible from the house," Pen said; " I rather think we are."

" Never mind; the professor will be poring over his books," replied Judy reassuringly. " But you wait here while I go and prospect."

She returned in a few moments.

" The door is locked, but I took a squint in at the windows; it seems to be a wood shed and is quite tidy, so I imagine it is in use. We had better try the other."

The second shed was a few yards further back and they approached it, keeping under cover as much as possible. It certainly looked a derelict place, with one small dirty window. The door was fastened by a latch and a padlock. On finding that the padlock was only half closed the girls removed it, and lifting the latch, entered. They looked round cautiously. Old cans, old flower pots, jam jars, a broken coal scuttle and some wooden boxes were all they saw at first; then, getting used to the dim light, they became aware of two eyes gleaming at them from a corner. It was the monkey.

"There he is," whispered Judy. "Now what shall we do?"

The monkey had no hesitation in knowing what he would do for, dashing to the door, he was out of the shed like a flash.

"Help!" cried Judy. "He's gone."

"We must hunt for the things quickly while he is away," urged Pen, going over to some old cans and peering into them. Yet, look as carefully as they could, nothing came to view.

"He may hide them somewhere else and not in the shed at all," said Judy in a disappointed voice.

Pen would not give up hope.

"This is much the likeliest place," she insisted.

So they set themselves to search again. Just when they were about to admit defeat, Pen caught her foot in a piece of sacking in the corner where the monkey had been sitting and fell, putting out her hands to save herself. As she did not rise immediately Judy asked:

"Are you hurt?"

Pen answered in an excited voice:

"No, but there are all sorts of knobbly things under these sacks; I do believe we've found his hoard."

Sure enough they had for, on removing two or three sacks, they found an extraordinary collection. There were brooches, tie-pins, cuff-links, wristlet watches, a miscellaneous assortment of seals, teaspoons, silver thimbles, a fountain pen, two small clocks, numerous trinkets and two rings. Judy pounced on one of the rings.

" Here it is, Pen! Here is Gracie's ring!" she exclaimed.

" Did you ever?" gasped Pen. " And where on earth could he have got all these things from? We had better collect them and take them back to Miss Edgar."

They filled their coat pockets with the various articles, and cautiously left the shed.

" Oof!" ejaculated Judy. " It's good to get into the fresh air again, isn't it? After you moved those sacks, the atmosphere was dreadful."

" I wish we could pull that ladder of ours over the wall," Pen said, as they made their way along the garden. " We will have to go right out into the open near the house before we reach the gate."

Judy was too much elated to feel any anxiety on that score. The ring was safe, and a great load had been lifted from her. It was just as they were creeping back into the shrubbery, the dangerous part safely passed, that they were arrested by a voice saying:

" May I inquire the reason for this unwarranted

trespassing on my property?"

They turned round startled and saw a middle-aged man, with field-glasses in his hand, and knew that he must be Professor Latham.

Judy found her voice first.

"I'm afraid we are trespassing," she began, "but we have done no harm."

"Then why skulk like thieves behind sheds, trees, and shrubbery?" he retorted. "Yes, I have been watching you, and I shall be much interested to see what it is that makes your pockets bulge as they are doing. Come into the house at once, and do not attempt to get away."

There seemed to be no alternative, so the girls followed the angry man into his library. In spite of the turmoil of their emotions, they could not keep from looking at one another in amused astonishment at the state of the room. Books lined the walls; books were piled on the floor, allowing only a narrow passage to the shelves; and there seemed to be books on nearly every chair. Round the table at the window, however, there was some clear space, and it was to this spot that the professor led his captives.

"Now empty your pockets," he commanded.

"Won't you listen to our explanation, first?" Pen pleaded.

"After you have done as I tell you," he replied firmly.

So out all the things were brought and laid on the library table. While they were thus occupied the professor took a letter from his pocket. It was from police headquarters, and stated that his report of missing articles had been duly received. It ended by saying that suspicion was centring round two young women who had been known to have called at certain houses in the district, professing to be collectors for charities. The one was tall and slim, the other smaller, and very fair. After reading this he put it back into his pocket, and turned to examine the articles on the table. He pounced at once on the bunch of seals and the fountain-pen. "The police are looking for these," he said.

While he was examining the seals intently Judy, pretending to arrange the things in some order, picked up Miss Lawson's ring and slipped it into her pocket. Why should she be deprived of the thrill of giving it back at once? If the professor was going to call the police in, the whole affair would pass into other hands.

Apparently satisfied that his bunch of seals was intact, the professor turned once more to the girls.

"Now," he said, "perhaps you will answer a few questions. First of all how did you get into my garden?"

"We came over the wall from the school," Pen said.

" And thought you would escape nicely, without any one seeing you, I suppose?"

" We didn't," cried Judy hotly; but, catching a warning look from Pen, she calmed down and nodded her head, in agreement with Pen's un-spoken suggestion that she would do the explain-ing.

The professor seemed in a suspicious mood.

" I see that you have some story concocted between you," he said, but I warn you that I am going to get at the truth."

Pen flushed.

" Of course we'll tell you the truth," she pro-tested, and she tried to explain their movements.

When she had described their findings of the monkey's hoard, her explanation, even to her own ears, sounded more like a made-up story than the truth. This was evidently what the professor thought, for he looked at her keenly and said :

" Do you really expect me to believe this fantastic story of a monkey living on my premises and stealing my possessions? Why have I not seen it, and where does it come from? I am unaware that any such animal has escaped from the zoological gardens."

" I'm sorry you don't believe the story," faltered Pen. " I know it sounds a bit queer, but it's true all the same."

The professor thought for a moment or two in silence, and then said:

" I propose you accompany me to the shed and show me this interesting thief. You have no objection, I presume?"

" Oh! no," replied Pen who then stopped and looked confused.

" I am afraid he isn't there now," she added.

" Very convenient of him," replied the professor sarcastically.

This was too much for Judy. She broke in heatedly:

" He's not there because he escaped when we opened the door; but if you are determined not to believe a word we say, ring up the school; they will tell you there that we are not thieves."

Professor Latham regarded her indignant face gravely. Then he said:

" If you are as honest as you try to make out, why did you take that diamond ring just now and put it in your pocket?"

So he had seen her after all! Judy flushed crimson, and did not know what to say; any explanation she could give might only increase the professor's suspicion.

Pen was not daunted.

" Judy wants to give that ring back to the person it belongs to," she said clearly.

" She may rest assured that all these things will

be returned to their rightful owners," he replied.

"Yes, but you don't understand," persisted Pen. "Judy was the last person to see that ring before it disappeared; and it's so horrid for her—it looks as if she had taken it. So now that we have found it, of course she wants to give it back herself."

"Before the police are put on the job, eh?" The professor's voice was dry, but there was a kindly look in his eye. He was beginning to like these two girls, and had long ago dismissed the thought that they might be the young women referred to in the police communication. He liked the way the tall slim one stood up for the cheeky one with the carroty curls. He decided to ring up the school before doing anything further. His hand was on the telephone, when the door opened and Dr. Clerk entered the room.

"Well, Latham, I've seen your cook; she got a touch—— Hullo! what's happening here, and why are my two patients looking so distressed?" He surveyed the scene with interest.

The girls' faces brightened.

"Oh! Dr. Clerk," cried Judy, "you'll tell him we aren't thieves, won't you?"

Once again they told their story of the monkey's secret hoard, the doctor listening in amazement.

"But what made you suspect that a monkey was the thief?" he asked.

"Pen, we've forgotten to tell about your

adventure last night," cried Judy, " and it's really the most important bit."

Pen recounted her experience of the night before, and both men listened intently.

" Ever heard of monkeys being attracted to bright things, professor?" inquired Dr. Clerk.

" Well, I've known of things being snatched from people who went too near a cage; and I can quite conceive that a monkey might be trained to be a thief," he answered. " But I can't understand how the little brute came to be shut up in my shed."

He looked inquiringly at the girls. Pen hesitated, then said:

" We don't want to get any one into trouble; but we heard that there was a monkey being kept in your shed."

The professor was content, evidently, to leave it at that, and not to question them further; no doubt he knew he would get to the bottom of the matter when he began his investigations. He decided that all the stolen articles should be displayed in his dining-room, and that those who had lost anything should come and identify their belongings.

" I shall have to let the police know about this," he remarked, " because there may be things here belonging to members of other households besides ours, and, anyway, I have already notified them of my losses. You girls are able to recognize some things, I know; but nothing must be touched until to-morrow."

He glanced at Judy and then added:

" Shall we send a special message by this young lady to the teacher who lost her ring?"

Judy beamed at him, and then Pen reminded them of possible danger.

" The monkey may come to-night and steal them all again," she pointed out.

" Bless me! The brute is still at large; I forgot that," exclaimed the professor. " It is a pity you girls let him out of the shed."

" We shouldn't have found anything, if he hadn't gone," countered Judy.

" Well, every window shall be firmly barred to-night," promised the professor, as he bade them good-bye.

The girls returned to The Elms in a very excited frame of mind.

The first person they met on entering the hall was the Head.

Chapter 10

ALL'S WELL THAT ENDS WELL

MISS MARTIN had arrived back only an hour before, and had been listening to Miss Edgar's report on the recent happenings.

Her thoughts of Judy were none too cordial; in fact she was very much worried. It was not that she thought for a moment that her niece knew where Miss Lawson's ring was, but she wondered when Judy was going to give up her irresponsible ways and behave as a girl of her age should. Did she not know that she was already in disgrace over the paper-chase? Why add to the score against her this new piece of thoughtlessness? Or did she not care? Now to make matters worse, she and Pen, who was supposed to be out only for a short time, had disappeared, not telling any one where they were going or asking permission, and had stayed away so long as to miss tea and to cause Miss Edgar real anxiety. Therefore, as her eyes lighted on the excited faces of the two girls, a feeling of annoyance passed over her, and her voice was cold when she spoke.

"What is the meaning of this, girls? Where have you been?"

Judy's cry of, "Aunt Bee, you're back," died on her lips; and Pen, feeling most uncomfortable, answered in a low voice:

"We've been next door."

The telephone rang in the study behind her, and Miss Martin turned back to answer it.

"Go up to the sick-room, both of you," she ordered, "and wait there until I come."

"Well," said Judy ruefully, as they stood looking out of the window, "I don't feel such a hero now. Do you, Pen? Who would think that we were discoverers of hidden treasure? For such a small person, it's wonderful how devastating Aunt Bee can be, isn't it?"

Pen laughed.

"I somehow never think of her as small," she replied. "She's really so—so big. I'm sorry we've worried her, she looks tired."

"I expect she is tired after sitting up so much with Aunt Maud. And it's me that has been worrying her for a long time, I know. Help! Here she is coming along the passage, I believe."

It was not Miss Martin who entered the room; it was Mrs. Philips with a tray.

"I don't know that you girls deserve any tea," she said sternly. "Pen, do you realize that you were only to go out for a short time? What the doctor would say if he knew of your doings, I can't think."

Judy chuckled.

"We've just been speaking to Dr. Clerk," she said, "and he is quite pleased with Pen."

Mrs. Philips looked sceptical.

"Shut that window down," she commanded. "Fresh air is all very well; but it is getting chilly now, and you must both be careful still. I don't want to have to nurse you again, I can assure you."

"We just thought we would lay in a supply for to-night, in case Aunt Bee issued an order that all windows were to be shut top and bottom," remarked Judy casually.

"I don't understand in the least what you are talking about," Mrs. Philips replied, "and I should be very much surprised if Miss Martin ever suggested such a thing. It seems to me," she added, "that, for girls in disgrace, you are much too frivolous."

"Disgrace!" cried Judy. "You wait. Our disgrace will soon be turned into—into applaudation!"

Mrs. Philips left the room in dignified silence.

Pen giggled.

"What a word, Judy!" she said.

"Well, I couldn't think of the right one. What

is the opposite of disgrace, any way?"

They had just finished their tea when the door opened again.

This time it was the Head. Miss Martin seated herself in an easy chair by the window, and the girls knew at once that she was no longer cross.

"Professor Latham has been speaking to me over the telephone," she began. "He has been telling me a most extraordinary story."

"It's all true, Aunt Bee," cried Judy eagerly. "We found all the things, and among them Gracie's ring—Miss Lawson's ring, I mean," she corrected herself hurriedly.

Miss Martin overlooked the impropriety and demanded the details from the beginning.

"You had better be the spokesman, Pen," she said, "as you seem to have been the principal actor in the drama."

She listened intently, stopping the narrative once or twice to ask a question.

"There is a saying that truth is stranger than fiction," she remarked, "and such happenings as these certainly go to prove it. It was a nasty experience for you, Pen, and we are all grateful to you for your courage in turning on the light; otherwise the thief might never have been detected. But what made you think of looking for the monkey in Professor Latham's shed?"

Pen hesitated for a moment, then answered:

"We didn't give the professor a full explanation, because we didn't want to get Lena into trouble; but I have been wondering whether it's right to keep quiet about it."

Then she repeated what Mary had told them.

"I can understand your reluctance to speak of the matter," Miss Martin replied, "but I think this ought to be known. I fear Lena's young man may not be all that she takes him for."

"No one knows where the monkey is now, and he'll be prowling about to-night, I expect," Judy put in. "Professor Latham is going to snib all his windows."

"We had better follow his example," replied the Head. "I do not want any one else to get a scare. I will tell the school at prayers to-night that the mysterious thief has been tracked and the stolen things found. Miss Lawson will be back by then; it will be a great relief to her. There is the bell. You had better go to preparation, Judy. Come to me after prayers, and I will tell you about Aunt Maud. Yes, she is recovering now. I would have come back here to-morrow or the next day, even if I had not received such an alarming letter from Miss Edgar."

When the door closed behind Judy, Miss Martin turned to Pen.

"I am so glad to find you better, and I want to

thank you for what you did for Judy in rescuing her from the bog. But, my dear child, why did you allow Dr. Clerk and myself to entertain the false belief that it was Judy who had saved you?"

" Well, you see," replied Pen, " you both seemed to take it for granted."

" The mistake was due to your friend, Mr. Saw. I understand quite well now how it occurred. I received a letter from him, redirected to me from the school, expressing the hope that *my niece, Miss Swanson,* had recovered from her exertions in pulling her friend out of the bog. As soon as I read that sentence, the mistake was at once accounted for. He must have heard you call me ' Aunt Barbara ', for, on thinking back over his conversation that afternoon, I remember he seemed to be puzzled that I was not your mother's sister. But all this does not explain why you allowed us to believe a story that was false."

Pen flushed.

" I knew Judy would tell you herself," she answered.

Miss Martin looked keenly at her.

" So she did, I am glad to say; but not at once."

" But she hadn't much chance to tell you at first," Pen explained earnestly. " And then you were so anxious about your sister that she didn't want to worry you."

" She is fortunate in having you to plead for

her," Miss Martin replied.

Then Pen, in some trepidation, put into words what had been in her mind ever since the accident.

" This won't mean that Judy can't enter for the water gala, will it? Please let her."

Miss Martin shook her head.

" No, Pen, it is no good your pleading for that. Breaking bounds is only one among many factors in the case; Judy knows that."

So Pen had to be content with the hope that perhaps Judy would not mind quite as much now.

There was great excitement in the school that evening while the Head was telling them about the monkey and his thefts. When she went on to say that, as it was still at large, it would be wise to keep their windows shut and snibbed that night, Judy looked across at Mrs. Philips and grinned openly, her eyes dancing with mischief. Miss Lawson was greatly relieved about the safety of her ring, and smiled quite graciously at Judy as the girls filed out of the room. Afterwards, upstairs in the recreation-room, Pen and Judy were bombarded with questions from both Seniors and Juniors.

" Is my watch there?" " Did you see my clip, Pen?" " Judy, is my pendant safe?" " I say, Pen, it must have been fearsome when he snatched your clock; it would have scared me stiff. I wonder you dared turn on the light." "Tell us again about the Professor."

When the clamour died down, Judy said to Pen in a low voice: "I'm going to see Aunt Bee."

What Miss Martin said to Judy at that interview, and what Judy said to her, none of the girls ever heard; but she went up to bed long after "lights out", and spoke to no one.

The next day she confided a little in Pen.

"You are quite right," she began, "Aunt Bee is big, Pen, bigger and finer than I ever knew. We had a great talk last night, and I told her all about my jealousy of you, and of how horrid I had been to you ever since you came. The funny thing was that she seemed to know about it. I believe there is mighty little that goes on in the school that she doesn't now. She was awfully decent about everything; gave me a fine old wigging about the pond, and evidently thought it a good opportunity to mention a few other things besides. Of course it's all up about the gala; but I expected that. It's quite right too; I've slacked abominably this term. I told her that she should see you dive, and she was quite interested; so you may be asked to give an exhibition, one of these days."

"Oh, no!" cried Pen, in distress. " I don't want to, Judy. There are others who could take

your place in the gala. Eileen is very good, I
know."

"Not in the same class with you, Dora says,"
declared Judy. "And you must do it, old girl, for
the sake of the school. Aunt Bee was a brick
about the ring, although she said that I should
not have touched it. When I told her it was an
answer to our prayers that you discovered about
the monkey, you should have seen her face!
Then I told her *everything,* and she is so glad
about it. I feel I never knew Aunt Bee before last
night. And another thing," continued Judy,
gurgling, " she told me Gracie was leaving at the
end of the term. She seemed to know that she
wasn't liked. Then she said: 'I have often
wondered why you girls give Miss Lawson the
nickname of Gracie; the others, of course, are
quite obvious!' When I told her it was because
the vicar preached a sermon on the first Sunday
she was here on St. Paul as a son of the Law
and a son of Grace, you should have heard her
laugh, Pen. She said: What ridiculous things
girls are! If her name had been Grayson, you
would have called her Lawrie, I suppose?' Think
of Aunt Bee saying that!"

The next morning, all those who had lost any
belongings went next door to identify them, and
Professor Latham told them that a man with a
monkey had been arrested early that morning.

It seemed that he had trained his pet to steal; and he had confessed to several hauls obtained in that way. So Lena was well rid of her young man.

By the midday post Pen received a letter from Nan enclosing a folder about the camp. She showed it to Judy, and they decided to take it to Miss Martin that evening and ask her whether they might go. Pen was returning to school the following day, and was to move out of the sick-room that night. Judy consulted with the girls in number eight and they decided to have a celebration.

" I'll speak to Cook," she promised, " and see if I can persuade her to make us some waffles. I'll explain that Pen and I missed our share on the paper-chase day; I know how to get round her. Mary will get them upstairs for us; she'll do anything for Pen since she found Aunt Bee's spoons for her. Don't breathe a word to any one, though; we don't want visitors."

Judy had forgotten her own assertion that the Head knew everything that went on in the school; and she might have received a shock if she had gone down to the kitchen after tea, and seen Miss Martin talking to Cook. She was telling her about her sister's accident.

" Don't let me interrupt you, Nannie," she said. (She called her by the old childish name when they were alone.) " What are you making?"

" Waffles."

Now waffles were only made on high days and holidays.

" Is it any one's birthday?" inquired the Head mildly.

" Not that I know of," answered Cook.

" Are you making them for the Staff?"

" No."

" I hope you are not aiding and abetting insubordination, Nannie," Miss Martin said sternly.

Cook covered over with a wet towel the batter she was beating.

" Now, Miss Barbara," she said, " don't you go and ask awkward questions. And if I were you I'd keep away from room number eight to-night. Those two poor lambs haven't had much fun these last few weeks."

So that was it, was it?

After supper Pen and Judy knocked at the Head's door.

" May we come in, Aunt Bee?" asked Judy.

" Surely," Miss Martin replied. " No more adventures to report, I trust?"

" No, and there wouldn't have been the last one if Prince had stayed with us instead of going away with you. Would there, old boy? You wouldn't have allowed a monkey to wander all over the school, I know," and she bent to pat the dog.

Prince welcomed both his friends, and Pen remembered that first night of her arrival. Did Judy remember it also, she wondered.

"It's about a summer camp, Aunt Barbara," she began. "Nan has asked me to go, and Judy would like to come too. This is the folder about it."

Miss Martin examined the pages and then said:

"It should be very interesting; both helpful and jolly too. I see that they will go in for camp-fire talks and choruses; but I notice one new item," and she read out, 'Sausage sizzle at Cove Point'. It sounds appetizing; we never had that."

"Were you ever at a camp?" asked Judy in surprise.

"Yes, indeed, and so was Pen's mother. They are splendid things."

Then turning to Pen, she said:

"You will be glad to see Nan again; are you sure that you want Judy to go too?"

"Quite sure," returned Pen.

If the Head had any doubt about the sincerity of the answer, the look that passed between the two girls would have banished it. How glad she was to see them such good friends! And to know that Pen had led Judy to a deeper Friendship filled her with thankfulness!

"Then I think it will be a fine experience for

you both," she said. "You had better write away for registration forms at once."

As they left the room, she murmured:

"Don't eat too many waffles."

Judy's face was a study, and Pen exclaimed, as she shut the door:

"Whatever does she mean?"

She knew later that evening, when a plate of waffles was produced, and also lemonade in which her health was drunk with great enthusiasm.